The Legend of Zoey

The Legend of Zoey

a novel by

candie Moonshower

DELACORTE PRESS

Published by Delacorte Press
an imprint of Random House Children's Books
a division of Random House, Inc.
New York

DELACORTE PRESS and colophon are registered trademarks of Random House, Inc.

www.randomhouse.com/kids

Educators and librarians, for a variety of teaching tools, visit us at
www.randomhouse.com/teachers

Library of Congress Cataloging-in-Publication Data
Moonshower, Candie.
The legend of Zoey : a novel / by Candie Moonshower. — 1st ed.
p. cm.
Summary: The diaries of thirteen-year-old Zoey, who lives in modern-day Tennessee, and Prudence, who lives in 1811 Missouri, tell how the two girls survive the New Madrid earthquakes and the subsequent floods after Zoey travels back in time.
ISBN-13: 978-0-385-73280-2 (trade) — ISBN-13: 978-0-385-90298-4 (glb)
ISBN-10: 0-385-73280-5 (trade) — ISBN-10: 0-385-90298-0 (glb)
1. New Madrid Earthquakes, 1811–1812—Juvenile fiction. [1. New Madrid Earthquakes, 1811–1812—Fiction. 2. Earthquakes—Missouri—New Madrid Region—Fiction. 3. Earthquakes—Tennessee—Fiction. 4. Time Travel—Fiction. 5. Chickasaw Indians—Fiction. 6. Choctaw Indians—Fiction. 7. Indians of North America—Fiction. 8. Diaries—Fiction.] I. Title.
PZ7.M7813Leg 2006
[Fic]—dc22
2005034954

The text of this book is set in 12.5-point Baskerville MT.

Book design by Angela Carlino

Printed in the United States of America

10 9 8 7 6 5 4 3 2 1

First Edition

For my husband,
Carl Lee Johnson,
with love

ACKNOWLEDGMENTS

Thanks to my critique groups—the Story Board: Lisa Albert, Kimberly Campbell, Barbara Greene, Syrl Kazlo, Susan Turner Mathew, Sandy McBride, Eileen Reiss, Kathy Witt, and Roxyanne Young; and my Nashville BRATs: Shirley Amitrano, Joanne Mamenta Bjordahl, Karen Carroll, Kim Noller, and Linda Ragsdale.

For their help and encouragement, I want to acknowledge Michael Burgin, Dr. Larry Mapp, Tracy Barrett, Susan Rhinehart Parham, Danna Stamper, Anastasia Porter, Kate Seregny, RN, and my mother and my brother, Judith Browning Knapp and Jack Browning.

Special thanks to Mary Wade, Sue Alexander, and the other fine folks in SCBWI. At Delacorte Press, thanks to Michelle Poploff and Wendy Loggia for requesting my manuscript, and to Emily Jacobs, who began the editorial process with me. To my outstanding editor on this project, Jodi Keller: I appreciate your patient guidance. Thanks also to my wonderful agent, Ginger Clark.

Much love and gratitude to my children, David Moonshower and Jack and Chloe Johnson, who were patient while Mom was "being a typewriter."

Journal of Zoey

(on being 13 and other important facts)

November 23, Saturday

I turned thirteen today. Finally! I'd been dreading my birthday for weeks, because of the current situation with the Parents, but it turned out all right. We went to Grandma Cope's house and celebrated the way we have every year of my life.

Mom and Dad let me take Jillian along. I think they wanted another body there to keep things normal. But that's okay. Even though she has gotten on my last nerve since seventh grade began, I love Jillian to death. We've been friends since our diaper days at the Rainbow of Peace Preschool.

Anyway, we were all at Grandma Cope's acting like everything was normal, which was hard. Nothing has been normal for a while now. It was time to open presents (the best part!), and I opened a bag from Grandma Cope and found this gorgeous journal that I'm writing in right now.

The outside is a light brown leather and has colored

beads sewn on it in a design that looks like a river flowing through a forest, with a guy riding a horse beside the river. In the sky is a shooting star, I think, but Grandma might have sewn too many layers of beads on one side. It looks kind of lopsided. But I'd never say anything. "This is so cool, Grandma!" I said, and meant it.

"What kind of design is that?" Jillian asked.

"I combined beadwork patterns from the Choctaw and Chickasaw tribes." Grandma Cope laughed her rusty-sounding laugh. "Something I learned from my grandmothers."

I fingered the beads. "You love rivers, don't you?"

"Yes." Grandma looked at me. "Rivers are the lifeblood of the land. Rivers take us away, and rivers bring us home."

Sometimes Grandma Cope says deep stuff I don't understand.

"Grandma Cope lived near the Mississippi when she was a little girl," Mom said for Jillian's benefit.

"Yes, in Chickasaw Country." Grandma always calls West Tennessee Chickasaw Country even though it hasn't been called that for almost two hundred years.

"Who's the man on the horse?" I asked her.

"That's a Chickasaw chief." Grandma's eyes twinkled. "And that's a mule."

Jillian and I took one look at each other and burst into laughter. "Mule Day!" we both shouted. In sixth grade, our social studies teacher, Ms. Simpson, took us to

Columbia, Tennessee, Mule Capitol of the World, for Mule Day. Who'd ever think of celebrating a *mule*?

"Why would an Indian chief be riding a mule?" I asked Grandma Cope. "Wouldn't he be on a fast stallion?"

"A stallion is fast. A mule is strong. For a long journey, a chief might decide a mule served him better." Grandma smiled.

All the talk of mules and journeys began to bore me. "How about some cake?" I said to Grandma Cope.

She gave me one of those piercing looks of hers. I guess I never realized that mules are one of her favorite things.

"Yes, let's have cake," Mom said. "I've got to head over to Mrs. Brady's house soon. Her baby might come today."

"Oh, great," I mumbled. Mom must have heard me, because she shot me one of *her* looks. But I didn't care! This was *my* birthday. I didn't like the thought of sharing it with some squalling newborn.

Dad patted my arm, but I could tell by how he was biting his lip that he was mad, too. Mom and Dad separated after Mom quit her nursing job to be a midwife. During one of their last arguments before Dad moved out, I overheard Dad tell Mom that he resented her throwing away her career to birth babies. Mom hollered that she was pursuing her *calling*. Dad hollered back that he guessed he would never pursue *his* calling. I didn't even know he had a calling. I thought he liked being an accountant.

Mom bustled into the kitchen and reappeared with my cake. The candles were burning. Everyone sang "Happy Birthday" to me.

"Time to make a wish!" Jillian said.

I closed my eyes and wished that Dad would move back home. I blew out all the candles with one big puff, but I didn't have much hope that my wish would come true. I'm thirteen now, and it's time to get over birthday wishes, shooting stars, and junk like that.

But I love my new journal. Grandma Cope always seems to know just what I need.

November 25, Monday

Today in social studies we talked about the geography of Tennessee—so boring. I do not care how many rivers run through Tennessee, or that we live in one of the top states in the country for camping and fishing. Rivers mean nothing to me. I hate camping and I detest fishing. Camping is just a weird way to be separated from indoor plumbing.

And fishing is just as bad. My counselor tried to teach me how to fish at Girl Scout camp one year and I hated it. It's smelly and disgusting. I'd rather sit around listening to Grandma Cope's olden-days stories all summer than go camping or fishing!

But I digress.

Social studies is still my favorite class of the day, though, because I do like history, and Ms. Drummond talks more about history than she does about social studies, whatever that is. Robbie Jamison and Quentin Williams are in my class, and so is Mike MacPherson. Mike's not as cute as Robbie, but he's smart, and he knows some weird stuff. I remember weird stuff, too, but I try not to advertise it.

"We're going on a two-day field trip next month," Ms. Drummond said at the end of class as we were all trying to stuff our junk into our backpacks without her seeing us. She hates it when we don't wait for the bell to ring to pack up. "We'll travel to West Tennessee to see Reelfoot Lake in Obion County, a lake formed during the New Madrid Earthquakes of 1811 and 1812."

"Yeah, but what'll we do that's fun?" Quentin asked. Everyone laughed.

"I'm glad you asked. We'll take a steamboat ride on the Mississippi. The first steamboat that traveled down the Mississippi was the *New Orleans*. Nicholas Roosevelt and his wife were on the river when the earthquakes struck the area. Roosevelt built boats and was the grand-uncle of future president Teddy Roosevelt."

The bell rang and we started rushing toward the door.

"Hang on! The cost of the trip is one hundred dollars, and we need some parent chaperones," Ms. Drummond shouted. "Take these permission slips home."

"I bet Mom'll be glad to get me out of her hair for a few days," I said to Jillian as we headed to lunch. "She says I've been 'sullen and uncommunicative' lately. What does she expect?"

"I'm sure she'll want you to have fun," Jillian said.

"I guess so," I said, "and Reelfoot Lake is better than nothing."

November 26, Tuesday

The trip to Reelfoot Lake will be an educational one, Ms. Drummond has hurried to assure us, and now I'm dreading it. We're going to study the flora and fauna; the topography, geography, and geology; and the history of the peoples.

Yes, she said it exactly like that: *the peoples.* Plural. Teachers are so weird. I should've known this trip wouldn't be about shopping or even something cultural like going to a play. Ms. Drummond even said "no modern conveniences."

"We'll learn about the lives of the Native Americans who lived in West Tennessee," Ms. Drummond said, "and the aftereffects of the New Madrid Earthquakes of 1811 and 1812."

I squirmed when she said that. I hardly ever think of Grandma Cope as being part of "the peoples," or even being Native American, until some teacher gets all serious about it in school. Sometimes teachers come right out and ask me about my "heritage" and embarrass me. I hate feeling different. I mean, technically speaking, I'm only about a quarter Native American, which hardly counts. Does it?

"When the earthquakes hit, the Mississippi ran

backward, and many Chickasaws drowned in the lake that was formed, which is now named after their chief."

"Awww!" several of the girls said. It does sound sad, but gosh, that was a couple of hundred years ago.

After Ms. Drummond dropped that bomb, the bell rang.

Jillian and I headed to our lockers. "You think you should tell the class about Grandma Cope?" Jillian asked me. "Her being part Chickasaw and all?"

"Now, why would I want to go and do that?" Ms. Drummond might want me to bring Grandma Cope to school. Yikes! Who brings their grandmother to school?

"Grandma Cope's cool," Jillian said.

I don't know about that, but I still understand what Jillian meant. My grandma acts a little strange at times, and she is different looking, with her long hair braided like all the Indians wear theirs in old movies, but when it counts, she acts like a *real* grandma. That's more than I can say for Jillian's grandmother, who is the boss of a huge company. She still looks like she's Mom's age. She wears short skirts and high heels, and she likes to be called Myra! Grandma Cope wears regular grandma clothes, like sweat suits. And she likes to be called Grandma.

Prudence Charity Keeler, of Tennessee,

in the Year of Our Lord 1811

23 November

After another long day of nothing but rain, I could not endure one more moment in our cabin, sewing with Mama. I mumbled something about going to the outhouse and made my escape.

It was dark outside, but I know my way around. I walked to the barn and went inside to the stall where King George spends his nights when we can convince him to go in there. Tonight we had no trouble. He was tired of standing in the field with rain pouring off him.

I heard soft munching as the old mule ate his oats and hay. I ducked through two of the planks keeping him in his stall. I put my head against his massive chest, twined my fingers in his rough mane, and cried until I was spent. George, as was his usual way, ignored me except to stomp his back foot a couple of times.

"You are one of my only friends in Chickasaw Country," I told King George. *Besides Kalopin,* I added silently. "You are not even that handsome a fellow. And I know you cannot dance!" I laughed at my own silliness, but the pang of loneliness in my heart did not completely abate. Will I ever have the chance to go to a social gathering and meet young folks my own age? It doesn't seem so, stuck out in the middle of nowhere as we are. I suppose I can forget about dancing.

Since we moved to Chickasaw Country two years ago for Papa to minister to the Indians, there are no visits from neighbors, nor do I have regular schooling as I did in Knoxville; only what Mama provides. The nearest towns are Little Prairie and New Madrid, each a two-day ride away, and we only make the trip when we need supplies. I do have one friend in New Madrid, Lizzie Bryan, but I do not see her often. I have no social life now.

I knew Mama would be worrying over me, so after taking time to compose myself, I left the barn. The sky was clear and the moon had appeared. I stopped to look at the stars, and I spotted the comet.

Since March, a comet with two tails has been visible in the night sky. The last time my Chickasaw friend, Kalopin, visited us, in the spring, he said this bodes ill for us. And in the last few weeks, things *have* seemed strange to me. One morning, very early, Mama and I saw a large herd of deer running east right along with squirrels and raccoons and other small animals. And a few days ago, at the creek, the fish were jumping out of the water and up onto the bank! I never even had to throw a line into the water. I just walked along and put fish in my basket. Very strange indeed.

When I told Papa what the Chickasaws say about the comet, he called these fears nonsensical. But I don't know what to think. Papa has had a great deal of book learning. Kalopin has had only the schooling Papa provided. He has always seemed to know things instinctively. Which way is the right way?

25 November 1811

Mama is with child, just as I suspected. She looks peaked, and I thought her belly had grown a bit, but she had been keeping herself covered with a shawl, so it has been difficult to tell for certain.

Tonight, after supper, I found Mama in the barn looking through an old trunk. In it were many pieces of clothing for an infant, as well as some blankets and swaddling clothes. It was exactly the opportunity I needed, so I decided to forge ahead.

"Are you with child?" I asked Mama bluntly.

At first, I thought she might holler at me for my bad manners. Proper ladies do not ask about bodily functions, she has told me time and again. But things are not the same now as when we were in Knoxville and had the luxury of acting like proper ladies. Then Mama looked like she might cry. I went to her straightaway and put my arms around her. She was stiff, but then she put her cheek against mine and rubbed, as she did when I was a little girl.

"Yes, Prudence, dear," she said. "I am with child. I will need your help, I think, with Papa away so much."

"When do you think the baby will come?" I asked.

"February. I feel certain it will be here before spring."

"Maybe the baby will arrive in time for our day of thanks," I said. That would certainly be a reason to give thanks.

"Oh, Prudence, you do not know what you are talking about. That would be too early." Mama sighed. "Papa must come home and stay home!"

This made me feel silly, as though I am still a little child. I pulled away from Mama and left her rummaging through the trunk. Mama persists in acting as if I have the sense of a goat.

26 November 1811

Today, a most exciting occurrence! A trapper going through Chickasaw Country brought us letters. One is a letter for Mama from Papa. The other is a letter especially for me from my friend, Lizzie Bryan, in New Madrid. The letters have been sitting at the fort for a number of weeks. I was happy Papa sent them along with the trapper.

We settled in front of the fire. Mama read Papa's letter to me:

"Dear Grace and Prudence, I hope this finds you well and in good Christian spirit. I realize that you were both

downhearted when I left you last, but fear not. I will keep my promise to return home by Christmas Day, and perhaps sooner, if possible. The good Lord calls me to a higher duty than ever these days. I must answer His call. I pray daily for strength."

Papa wrote of other things that were solely for Mama. She did smile a bit when she finished reading the letter; then she folded it and placed it in her apron pocket. I noticed her touching the letter several times throughout the evening.

She seems to be in better spirits. For this I am glad.

My letter from Lizzie was mostly of girlish things. She is studying the pianoforte at the home of Miss Archer, and her art continues to improve. She says she is filling her marriage chest with embroidered linens and other things.

I read Lizzie's letter to Mama.

"It sounds as if Lizzie is in a hurry to be wed," Mama remarked. "Does she have a young man picked out yet?"

I could see by the way Mama's lips quivered that she found Lizzie's matrimonial plans amusing. I said nothing. We were quiet for a while. The only sounds were the clicking of Mama's knitting needles and the crackle of logs in the fireplace.

I felt so lonesome just then that a little sob hitched in my throat, but I caught myself in time and swallowed it. I turned to look at the fire and blinked to stop the tears.

"Does Lizzie's letter make you so sad?" Mama asked me.

"I fear I will never marry," I blurted without thinking, "or do anything important in my life."

"Of course you will marry," Mama said, quite gently, which means that she is not as sure as she would have me believe.

"How will I meet any eligible beaux when there are no men within fifty miles of here?" I asked. My voice sounded petulant. I know I should not be sharp with Mama, but it seems ridiculous that she should encourage me. I used to think about marriage and keeping a house—before we came here. Now my life is chores and helping Mama, and waiting for Papa to come home.

"Perhaps before the baby comes, we might move to New Madrid," Mama announced. "I shall talk it over with your papa."

I must admit that my jaw dropped!

"You can go to school and to church, and I believe that there are some social gatherings there that are appropriate for nice young ladies."

"And there is the fort," I added.

Mama responded to this comment with a frown. She is a little unsure of soldiers.

"I mean to say that it is safer in New Madrid, with the fort," I said.

"Hmm." The corners of Mama's mouth turned up ever so slightly. "The Indians do not dare attack." Mama nodded with enthusiasm at her own logic. "I have not yet discussed this idea with Papa, but I believe with the baby coming, he will go along with it." Mama smiled at me. Her small hands smoothed the folds of her skirt.

My hopes began to rise. Then I thought of Kalopin. If we move to New Madrid, I might not see him at all. I hate the thought of leaving my one friend in Chickasaw Country, but the idea of living in New Madrid sounds like heaven to me.

I could feel my heart beating fast in my chest. Civilized society, schooling, church—I can enjoy all this again in New Madrid. I can have friends again, and, later on, beaux. I can go to school and do something with my life!

When I retired for the night, I dreamed of New Madrid. I wore a new frock and sat in a buggy behind a fine horse, instead of in the wagon behind King George. Two young men stood by the buggy and talked to me. They were young soldiers from the fort.

Zoey

November 28, Thanksgiving!

Turkey Day turned out to be a little tense—more like Turkey Vulture Day, since Mom and Dad insisted we spend the holiday together.

"You're a little early, Marissa," Grandma Cope said when she opened the door in her robe and slippers.

"Sorry, Mother. I thought we could help," Mom said to Grandma, a little snippily, I thought.

"Come on in, then," Grandma said, holding the door open.

"Has he arrived yet?" Mom asked, looking around the living room. I knew then that we had arrived an hour earlier than we needed to so that Mom could make sure we beat Dad there. Mom is always getting on to Dad about his "inability to be timely."

"Will you come and zip my dress, Zoey?" Grandma called to me on her way to her bedroom, ignoring Mom's question.

I went into Grandma Cope's cozy room. She keeps

the lamps covered with scented vintage hankies, so it's always dim in there, and it smells like eucalyptus.

"Shut the door," she said.

I shut the door.

"Have they been carping at each other?" she asked.

That's what I love about Grandma Cope. She never tries to gloss things over with pretty words.

"No, not much," I lied.

Grandma Cope gave me one of those piercing looks.

"Well, some," I admitted. "They keep going on about Mom's 'lifelong dream,' as she calls it. The last time they talked, Dad argued that he had dreams, too, but Mom said it was her turn to do what she wanted. That's all I heard before I put on my headphones and turned my music up." I sighed.

When Mom and Dad first separated, Grandma Cope told me that back in her day, people didn't worry about being fulfilled, and hardly anyone got a divorce. They stayed together for the sake of the children. Was it better that way? I've thought about that a lot.

"Hmm," Grandma Cope said, interrupting my thinking. She sucked in a deep breath, and I zipped her dress. On holidays, Grandma always stuffs her nice round body into a dress. I don't know why she doesn't wear jeans or sweatpants like she does every other day. She applied lipstick and put on some earrings that looked like miniature dream catchers. Then Grandma Cope sat on the edge of her bed and patted the spot beside her. I went to her and sat down.

"Zoey, I know that things seem dark now. But I believe that this is just a detour in your parents' journey through life."

I took a deep breath. For Grandma, every problem in life can be made into some kind of travel or automotive analogy—like impending divorce is just a bad transmission that needs overhauling.

Grandma Cope took my hands in her hard ones. "I have a feeling, Zoey. I feel like certain things will happen soon that will make your parents take a close look at their priorities," she said, her voice deadly serious. Of course, Grandma Cope almost always sounds deadly serious. Her grip on my hands was beginning to cut off my blood supply.

"Do not worry," she said. "With hard work, sometimes we can change things. Sometimes it is our destiny."

I looked up from my bloodless hands to Grandma's bloodless face. My heart about jumped out of my chest. Her eyes were rolled back in her head and she was kind of humming.

"Grandma! Grandma Cope, are you okay?" I asked her. I shook my arms until she let go of my hands, and then I patted her face. "Mom! Mom!" I shouted.

Grandma was still pale and her skin was ice cold. "A river will never lie to you, Laughing Eyes," she mumbled. At least, that was what I thought she said, but it was hard to tell because her words were slurred.

"What did you say?" I asked. She didn't seem to hear me.

"What's wrong, honey?" Mom asked as she rushed in.

"It's Grandma!" I said. "She told me something about rivers laughing at lies or something! It didn't make sense!"

Mom immediately sprang into nurse mode. She put her fingers to Grandma's throat and felt her pulse. That was when Grandma opened her eyes and looked around.

"I'm all right, Marissa," Grandma said. And she did look fine, if a little pale.

"We need to get you to a doctor," Mom said.

"Now, Marissa, quit bothering me. I'll see my doctor in January when I go for my annual checkup."

Just then, the doorbell rang. Mom and I looked at each other. I was worried about Grandma, and I could see that Mom was, too.

"That's Josh," Grandma said. "Someone get the door."

"Mother, you rest for a minute or two," Mom said. "Zoey, come with me and get a cool cloth for Grandma's head." I followed her into the living room.

Mom opened the front door. "Hello, Joshua," she said to Dad in that tone she uses when he shows up late, even though he was actually half an hour early.

"Hello, Marissa," Dad said, taking off his coat. Mom hung it in Grandma Cope's hall closet like he was a guest. Which, technically, I guess he is now, if we're not going to be a family anymore.

"Mother, I thought I told you to stay in bed!" Mom said to Grandma Cope, who was now in the living room.

"And I told you I feel fine." Grandma Cope gave Mom a sharp look, but then she walked over to Dad and gave him a big hug. I swear, I thought he was going to start bawling—and I thought I might, too. "Supper's about ready, Josh," she said in the same way she's said it every year that I can remember. That helped ease the big old lump that was in my throat.

I lit the candles while Dad began carving the bird. Mom helped Grandma Cope bring in the food, and there was a ton of it: casseroles, deviled eggs, and Indian pudding, not to mention the huge turkey stuffed with sage dressing, and pumpkin pies. Mom and I've been eating at Mambo Taco a lot with all of her midwife friends, and I miss home cooking—just not the organic, whole-grain meals Mom used to make. I guess she hasn't had the heart lately to fire up the food processor.

"Mother Cope, this looks like a meal fit for a king," Dad said, practically smacking his lips over the turkey.

Uh-oh. Mom must have been feeling kind of defensive, because she scowled at that.

I had to agree with Dad, though. I'd already sent up a prayer of thanks for Grandma Cope's cooking.

I ate until I thought I'd pop out of my jeans. I even saw Dad unsnap his when he thought we weren't looking. Mom didn't eat a thing. She'll be my size before too long.

As good as the food was, it didn't hide the fact that everything is different for our family now. I could tell that Grandma knows it, too. She had a funny expression on her face all through dinner. I wondered if she was really feeling as fine as she'd told us, or if all that cooking had taken more out of her than she was letting on. Tonight made me wonder how Christmas will be for us this year. I almost dread it.

Prudence

28 November, Day of Thanks 1811

Dear Papa is home! He returned, just as he promised. He arrived last night, tired and wet, and went straight to bed. He is pleased to be here to celebrate our day of thanks with us.

"I did not think you would make it back so soon," Mama said as she made Papa cozy by the fire today. She handed him a cup of coffee. "Will you stay home this time?"

"I must go and visit the Creeks, but I promised I would come home, and I have," Papa said, smiling. "As you get closer to your time, I will come home to stay," he added with a look at me.

"I know about the baby, Papa," I said.

Papa frowned, but only a little bit and only for a moment. "Well, that is good, then, I suppose. Are you taking care of your mother for me, Prudence?"

"Yes, Papa, I am," I said, proud that he was speaking to me as an adult.

"Thank you." Papa took a long sip of his coffee.

While Mama finished preparing our meal, I sat by Papa. I wanted to talk, but first I looked to see if Mama was listening.

"What is it, daughter?" he asked.

"Have you seen our friend Kalopin in your travels?" I asked in a quiet voice.

Papa glanced toward where Mama was setting our dishes out on the table.

"No," Papa said, "but I heard news of him when I was visiting the Choctaws. Apparently Kalopin went against Chief Copiah's wishes and stole Copiah's daughter, Laughing Eyes, to be his wife."

"He stole her? Is there some reason Chief Copiah would object to Kalopin's marrying his daughter?" I asked.

"He does not believe that Kalopin is worthy of Laughing Eyes," Papa said. "Because of his clubfoot."

"But it is hardly noticeable!" I said in quick defense of my friend. "Kalopin is one of the most worthy individuals I know. He is young, but he is a good chief, and a good trapper, and he provides well for his tribe. You have told me so yourself, Papa!"

"You should not be thinking about that Indian at all, Prudence," Mama said sternly. She had heard us.

"Kalopin is our friend!" I said. "Is he not, Papa?"

"Yes, he was our friend when he was a boy, but now he is a man. And he has made Chief Copiah very angry. If Copiah has his way, I am afraid that we will not see much of Kalopin in the future. Copiah says he has put a curse on Kalopin for taking Laughing Eyes. Nothing will come of it, but Kalopin would be wise to stay close to home."

How would I ever see him again?

Papa sat for a few moments and then took my chin in his hands and turned my face until I was looking at him. "Prudence, I talked with your mother last night. How would you like to spend some time in New Madrid this winter?" he asked me.

"Truly, Papa?" My heart beat excitedly. "Might we move there?"

"I do not know about moving permanently, but perhaps for the winter."

I looked at Mama. Her smile faltered a bit, but she nodded at me encouragingly.

"What are your thoughts, Papa?" I asked.

"I have been thinking that we might go for Christmas. We can find a nice place for you and Mama to stay until the baby comes. I would feel better knowing you were near other good people should you need help with anything."

"And I may go to school?" I asked.

"Yes, I think that is a good plan." Papa smiled at me, and his blue eyes twinkled. "You are growing up, Prudence. I know that we need to plan for your future."

I laughed. "I was beginning to think that you wanted me to remain a spinster my whole life, Papa," I said. "And there is so much I still would like to learn at school, too."

23

"Young folks need friends. I am certain it has been lonely for you here in Chickasaw Country."

I swallowed hard around the lump in my throat. "It was not so lonesome before, when Kalopin visited. But he has grown up and left. I suppose he does not need my friendship now."

"Prudence, dear, Kalopin is still your friend, and I feel certain that should you ever need him, he will be there for you. But just as you will grow up and make a life for yourself, Kalopin is making his own way. That is what God intended."

"Come to the table," Mama called.

Papa and I made our way to the table and sat down to our holiday meal. Mama had roasted an old hen that had quit laying, and a rabbit, and with these meats we had a few roasted potatoes, onions, turnips, and Indian corn from our root cellar. To preserve our flour, Mama and I had made fried bread from Indian cornmeal. Papa declared it a feast.

After dinner, Papa read aloud from the Bible. Then we went to our beds.

Even from my bed, I could still see the twin tails of the comet through the hole in the hides covering my window. I wish it would disappear.

2 December 1811

Papa left again this morning at first light. At dawn, I heard Mama and Papa rustling about, so I rose and poured myself coffee while Papa packed his bag. Mama looked as if she had been crying.

"I solemnly promise to return in time for Christmas," Papa said, putting his arms around Mama.

"You promise?" I asked him. "And we can go to New Madrid then?"

Papa laughed his jolly laugh. "Yes, for certain." Papa gave Mama a special look and squeezed her. I thought Mama might start to cry again, but she was strong.

Papa waved as he cantered away on his horse. I watched until I could no longer see him. I hope that Papa returns soon, but I have my doubts. Sometimes it seems as though Papa cares more for the Indians than he does for his own family. I feel that I am disloyal, but Mama and I need him to stay home with us.

I believe that Mama has doubts as well, for though she held him tight before he rode off, I sensed her anger. I know she is afraid of the Indians and wishes that Papa would not leave us alone so often.

Why must a man follow his own path even when it is contrary to what everyone else might need?

3 December 1811

Today, the sun was out, a rare and much-welcomed event, as it has been so rainy of late. I could not wait to get outside! There was a slight chill in the air, but the sun warmed me, inside and out.

As we did our chores, Mama stopped frequently and straightened her back.

"I can finish, Mama," I said. "You should go inside and rest." I had been dawdling, thinking about our move to New Madrid, and Mama had been doing most of the work. I hate for Mama to feel that I do not do my share, but it is most wearisome for me to be thinking of chores all the time.

"I know that you are doing your best." Mama sighed. A look of discomfort flashed across her face.

"Do you feel bad today?" I asked. I felt guilty for thinking only of myself.

"A bit." Mama wiped her forehead with her apron.

Looking at her, so pale and clammy and tired, I felt another flash of anger at Papa for leaving us to work so hard alone. He should be here helping us, especially now.

"Go inside and rest," I insisted. "I will finish up out here."

"There is no need. I must become accustomed to these pains and to the weariness."

"Why do women want to have babies when it makes them feel so poorly?" I asked. I figured that Mama would not answer since I was attempting to discuss personal matters, but she surprised me.

"It is the way of life, Prudence," she said. "Sometimes the outcome is sorrowful, but having a family is a joyful thing."

"And when this baby is born, we can celebrate," I said hopefully.

"I will not think about celebrating until and if the babe is old enough for schooling." She looked grim.

"But, Mama!" I started.

"Prudence, though you believe yourself to be a woman, some things are beyond your understanding. You know I have lost three other babies in the thirteen years since you were born. And now we are alone in this forsaken wilderness. . . . There is a good chance this babe will not live, either."

There is nothing to say. Mama is right; I do not understand.

Tonight, on the way to the barn to get King George and the other animals bedded down, I stared hard at the strange, two-tailed comet in the sky. I shivered thinking about Mama and the baby, and Kalopin's talk back in the spring about the comet. I cannot fathom what it all means, but I am frightened.

Zoey

December 2, Monday

Mom got called out tonight to assist at a birth, so she dropped me off at Grandma Cope's. She invites me to go with her sometimes, but all the waiting is boring. I'd rather go to Grandma's house.

I did most of my homework, but I stopped reading about halfway through the chapter Ms. Drummond assigned on the New Madrid Earthquakes and Reelfoot Lake. It was kind of interesting, I have to admit, but heck, we're going there in a couple of weeks. I'll learn all about it then. After I dumped everything back in my backpack, I wandered into the living room. Grandma Cope was looking at some old pictures.

"Would you like to look with me?" she said, patting the couch cushion beside her.

She smelled like the "calming" lavender powder Mom buys her for her birthday every year, and I snuggled up to her a little bit like I used to do when I was a kid. She opened up a completely moldy photo album.

On the first page was a picture of an old couple standing by a fence. They looked totally dour and watchful. The woman wore an apron that covered her from her neck to her knees. The man's pants were hiked up to his chest with suspenders, and he had on a straw hat.

I felt squirmy. These were exactly the kind of "peoples" Ms. Drummond is forcing us to learn about at school. And they're related to me. "Are those your great-grandparents?" I asked.

"They're my parents!" Grandma Cope laughed.

"Really? But they look ancient here," I said before I could stop myself. But they did!

Grandma Cope chuckled. "They were only in their fifties when this picture was taken. They lived a hard life."

"Yeah, I guess. What were their names again? Saffron and what?"

"My mother was named Saffron Cope. My father was John Bear Hunter."

"So how come your name is Cope instead of Hunter?"

"Bear Hunter," Grandma corrected me. "Most Indians in our tribes take their mother's names. Or they used to, at any rate."

"Mom didn't," I pointed out.

"When your mother came along, it seemed to be a new day. She took her father's name, Smith. We thought it might be better that way."

"Why?" I asked. I'd heard all this before, but it still didn't make any sense to me.

"Because your grandfather was a white man, and

American families used the man's name then. We didn't want your mother to feel different."

"I guess Mom couldn't figure out what to do when I came along," I said. "Since my name is Smith-Jones." I sighed. That made Grandma Cope laugh.

"Some of your mom's generation think equal credit should be given to both parents. I can't disagree with that."

I can. Having a name like Zoey Saffron Lennon Smith-Jones is a constant source of pain for me. If it wasn't bad enough having both parents' last names, they had to go and give me two middle names. They're not even regular names, but names Mom and Dad decided on during their college days when they were expanding their horizons or something.

I don't even pretend to understand what they were thinking, but Mom says they each picked a meaningful middle name. Lennon I understand, with their love for the Beatles, especially John Lennon. But why did they name me after Grandma's mother, Saffron?

Grandma turned the pages of the album. There were a lot of boring pictures of the farm she grew up on, some sad-looking cows and goats, and brothers, sisters, aunts, uncles, and various other people that even Grandma couldn't remember, mostly looking old and grumpy like her parents.

One picture caught my eye. It was of a young man, and he was handsome in an old-timey way. His black hair was parted in a severe fashion and slicked over, and he was wearing jeans and a T-shirt. His eyes were smiley and happy-looking, though, and he had some big arm muscles bulging below where his T-shirt sleeves were rolled up. "Who's that?"

"That was your grandfather Sam when he was very young."

"He was kind of cute, Grandma," I said. I'd only seen pictures of him with my mom when she was a baby.

She laughed. "All the girls were after Sam. But we knew we would marry from the first time we met when I started working for his mother. She never accepted our relationship, I'll tell you that."

I hesitated but asked the question I wanted to ask anyway. "Was it because you're Indian?"

"Yes. Sam's mother thought all Indians were poor and uneducated. Even though I never lived on a reservation and I'd graduated from high school, I was still not good enough."

"That's awful, Grandma!" I said. "Native Americans are just as good as anyone else!"

"Yes, you are." Grandma gazed at me with a strange look in her eyes.

That stopped me. What if someone thought less of me just because I'm part Indian? Luckily, no one really knows except Jillian and a few of my teachers from times when Grandma Cope has come to school to pick me up. Dad's family is from all over Europe, so I'm just a mix of stuff.

We looked at the picture of my grandfather for

another couple of minutes. "I wish I could have met him," I said.

"I wish your mother could have known him better, too. He died just after she was born, during an influenza outbreak."

"People can die from the flu?"

"Yes, but it doesn't happen much anymore. Back when I was young, though, many illnesses were deadly."

"Wow," I said, which seemed kind of like an understatement, but I'd never known how Grandpa died. "That must have been so sad for you, Grandma."

"It was, but I've had a happy life. Things happen the way that they are meant to happen."

I shook my head. "I don't believe that," I said. "Why should Mom have to grow up without a father? And now she's kicked Dad out, and I don't have a father around, either! How fair is that?"

Grandma Cope sat silent for a few minutes while I took a few of Mom's famous deep cleansing breaths. "I didn't say that life is fair. Just that it unfolds as it is meant to," she said.

None of that makes sense at all. What good is free will if things happen any old way and we don't have any control over them?

December 4, Wednesday

It's two o'clock a.m. and I still can't sleep, even though I've been in bed for ages. Tonight Mom and I went for tacos with some other midwives. They were all yakking about their workday. If their patients knew the kinds of personal details their midwives tell about them, they'd die of shock.

I hate hearing them talk about birthing and all that. It's kind of cool when I see it on *General Hospital*, my favorite soap, but it's all so *personal* when Mom and her friends discuss it. Like I'm right there during the action—and who wants to be there when someone has a baby? Yuck.

Anyway, we were hanging out at Mambo Taco and I was looking out the window, trying to tune out all the talk of labor pains and how many minutes apart they were, when I saw the comet with two tails. All the papers (and my teachers) were talking about it when it appeared out of nowhere in March. They said it's weird because it first showed up way back in the 1800s, but no one pays much attention to it now. My dad is completely obsessed with it, though, and reads all he can about it. When he found out we were going to Reelfoot Lake, he said that there was a two-tailed comet in the sky back when the lake was formed, too.

"And I could not believe that this woman didn't realize she was having twins until she was actually in labor. It astounded me!" That was Mom's friend, Norah, talking.

"Had you suspected twins?" Mom asked.

Norah shook her head. "She didn't call me until she was pretty far along. She looked bigger than normal, but not too out of the ordinary. I'm wondering if she ever saw a doctor at all!"

"So what happened?" Mom asked.

"After the first baby came, I went to rub her belly, and it was hard as a rock!" Norah laughed and sipped her drink.

All of a sudden, I felt like I was hearing everyone from inside a tunnel. Their voices were getting softer and softer. I tried to get my bearings by staring out the window and tuning them out.

But while I was looking at the comet—and I really was concentrating on it—I smelled this terrible odor, like rotten eggs or something. The weirdest part was that no one seemed to notice, or else they were trying really hard to ignore it.

The odor was so strong I felt like I was going to faint.

I poked Mom's leg under the table.

"What is it, honey?" she said.

"I feel sick," I said.

For a minute she looked at me like she didn't believe me. It's not like I make a habit of playing sick, but I have done it a couple of times in recent months to get out of going to school or hanging out with Mom's friends.

She put her hand on my forehead. "You do feel kind of clammy," she said, like she was surprised. "Maybe you ate a bad taco. How's your stomach?"

"Mom," I said. "I did *not* make that smell!"

"What smell?" she asked. Her eyes were wide and she looked completely innocent.

"Like someone needs to go to the bathroom," I whispered.

Mom took a deep breath. I could see that she was mentally counting to ten so that she wouldn't holler at me. "Are you nauseous?"

"No, I just feel kind of woozy from that awful stench!"

"Zoey, it smells fine in here. Maybe it was all that talk about childbirth. I don't see why it embarrasses you so much," Mom said. A little frown formed between her eyebrows, which is not good, because it means she's going to start obsessing on something. "Sometimes I wonder if you should hear all this."

"Forget it, Mom. I'm all right now." And I was. The awful smell was gone. I looked out the window and the comet was covered up by a dark cloud.

Prudence

7 December 1811

Today Mama and I arrived in New Madrid after a journey that has taken us two days from our home in West Tennessee. I was never so glad to get to civilization and see all manner of different people shopping, walking, and conversing with each other in a real town.

There were many young soldiers around, too, and as we were about to enter the general store, one of those young men doffed his hat and nodded as I passed. Of course, Mama would never allow me to speak with him, so I did not stop, but I could not help noticing how handsome he was in his uniform.

The last time we came to New Madrid was in the summer. Since then, Mama has put off coming without Papa, but we could not wait any longer. There are many things we need to purchase. The weather already hints of what is to come. Cold rains have been the rule.

Mama was worried that we would be attacked by Indians before we could cross the river, but all went well. I have practiced with Papa's old long rifle since he taught me how to shoot, and I am prepared to use it if I must.

When Mama was a child, her family lived in New York, and they were attacked by Indians. Even though the Indians we have known in Chickasaw Country are peaceful, she has never gotten over her fear of them. It upsets Papa and me greatly, but Mama cannot seem to shake her uneasiness about Indians—all Indians.

Inside the general store, we listened to the talk as we examined the merchandise. I stayed close to the counter, as I had my eye on some hard peppermint candy that I liked. I hoped Mama would let me purchase a penny's worth.

"The Indians I trade with are predicting a hard winter," Mr. Armando, the proprietor, said to the group of men standing at the counter with the scales for weighing skins and furs. "One of them Chickasaw mingos was in here earlier. He was talking about the wrath of the Great Spirit and all that Indian witchery."

A huge man with a long beard dressed in filthy leathers laughed. "I heard tell that the Choctaws around here are fighting mad at the local Chickasaws over something. They're saying they've put a curse or spell or something on some Chickasaw chief."

I wondered if they were talking about Kalopin. My stomach knotted at the thought.

A little wiry man with deep-set eyes and a red nose

spat on the floor and then kicked some sawdust over it. "All them savages are crazy acting, if you ask me," he said.

Most of the people standing around nodded, but I did not.

When the gossip turned to the threat of another war with England, I stopped listening. Mama was examining some pretty bolts of cloth. I wished she would purchase something new for winter, but I suspected that she would not. I was correct. After a few more minutes of looking, we left the general store.

Not that it truly matters whether I have a new dress, since I rarely see anyone now. I could go all winter in the same old frock and no one would be the wiser. I sighed, a little too loudly, I suppose, since Mama shot me a hard look. Even if we move to New Madrid, I know there is no money for new clothes.

Just as we came out of the store and began loading our goods into our wagon, I saw Kalopin. He was with a group of Indians—several older men and women, and a few young Indians, too. He has changed from a boy to a man since last he visited with us.

I must have been gaping at him, because Mama prodded me in the ribs with her elbow. But I could not help myself. He had a skin bag hanging around his neck on a leather string. His leather moccasins covered his bad foot. On his back was a bundle of skins.

"Good day, Mistress Keeler. Good day, Miss Keeler," he said in his deep voice as he reached down and hefted a sack of flour—the last of our purchases to load—into the wagon for Mama.

Mama nodded but did not look at Kalopin. She began to discourage Kalopin's visits to our cabin about a year ago. She says white women do not associate with savages. But Kalopin is not a savage. He is my friend. She and Papa have had words about this.

"Good day, Kalopin," I said. My voice sounded a little shaky in my ears. I felt a horrid blush creeping up my neck.

"How are you?" Kalopin asked. His English is very proper. Papa taught him. He looked at Mama. "How is Reverend Keeler?"

Mama did not speak. She climbed into the wagon and sat down with her back to us.

"Papa is fine. He is visiting the Creeks," I jumped in. "He said there was talk of you when he went to see Copiah."

"Yes, I have been to visit the Choctaws," Kalopin said with a smile, "under cover of night." He turned and stretched a hand back to the group of Indians and gently pulled forth a young woman of about his age. Her hair was dark, long and heavy, parted down the middle. She was not beautiful except for her eyes, which slanted upward slightly at the outside corners and were shiny onyx black.

"I traveled to Chief Copiah's tribe to take my bride," Kalopin said with pride. "This is Copiah's daughter, Princess Laughing Eyes. Soon we will marry."

I smiled at her, but my heart burned. Mama cleared her throat and shook the reins, which allowed me to say a hasty farewell. God bless Mama for that. I suppose Kalopin can no longer be my friend. He is to be married. He took Laughing Eyes, just as Papa said he would. I must stop now, for the tears come.

8 December

After purchasing our goods in New Madrid yesterday, we saw Mrs. Bryan and her daughter, my friend Lizzie. We had stopped at Dr. Stuart's house for a few medicinal supplies. Mrs. Bryan and Lizzie were enjoying a cup of tea there with Mrs. Stuart, who invited us to join them.

It was nice to be in the company of a girl my age, and Lizzie is always quite jolly, but my heart was still hurting from my encounter with Kalopin.

"How long will you stay?" Lizzie asked me, her green eyes sparkling.

"Not long enough to suit me," I replied. "I cannot believe how much the town has grown since we were last here." I had seen many new settlers walking the streets, both English- and French-speaking. New houses had sprung up all around the fort, and the sappy smell of recently cut lumber filled the air.

"Yes. Many new people have moved into the area," Lizzie said.

"Do you still go to school?" I asked.

"Yes," Lizzie said. She turned down her mouth. "I do not enjoy it, but Mother says that as long as a school is available to us, I must go."

"Oh, you are lucky," I said. "I have not been to school in ever so long."

"You do not have a school where you live?" she asked, her eyes wide with disbelief.

I understood her feeling. Even though Tennessee has been a state for fifteen years, we have no towns so fine as New Madrid, and it is in Louisiana, which is still a territory!

"We do not have a school, a church, or a general store," I told her. "I would love to live in New Madrid and go to school."

"Why does your family not move here?" Lizzie said.

"We moved to Chickasaw Country so Papa could minister to the Indians. But Papa said we might move soon. Mama . . ." I paused and looked over at my mother. Lizzie looked, too, and seemed to understand my meaning, because she smiled.

"What about beaux?" Lizzie asked with a glance at our mothers, who were chatting away over their teacups. Her voice was lower than before.

"There are no boys or young men where I live. How can I expect to have a beau?"

"Maybe you will meet someone in New Madrid." Lizzie laughed aloud, then covered her mouth with her hand. "I have brothers," she whispered. "They are young, but they are boys."

"Oh, Lizzie Bryan!" I cried. But I could not help thinking about the young soldier from the fort.

After tea, we made our way to the Bryans' house with Lizzie and her mother. They invited us to spend the night and attend Sabbath services with them today.

The new Methodist church was erected last year and boasts beautiful carved, polished wooden pews instead of rough benches. Papa left a church even nicer than this one when we moved from Knoxville. He says the ground below and the sky above are good enough for worshipping, but I must admit I enjoyed sitting on those pews!

The minister droned on and on until I felt my eyes begin to roll back in my head, but it was good to sit amongst people, and there was still the promise of Sunday supper with the Bryans after the service.

When we returned to the Bryans' house, the littlest children played outdoors while Lizzie and I helped our mothers prepare the table. Mr. Bryan sat with us, smoking his pipe and regaling us with news.

"Did you hear that Mr. Nicholas Roosevelt launched his new steamboat, the *New Orleans*?" he said to Mama and Mrs. Bryan. "They left Pittsburgh on the twentieth of October."

"I heard that his wife is accompanying him," Mrs. Bryan said as she mixed cornmeal and flour in a large bowl.

"Harrumph," Mr. Bryan said around the stem of his pipe.

Mrs. Bryan looked at Mama and smiled.

"I do not know why he would want to bring his wife on such a trip," Mr. Bryan said.

"I know why she would want to go," Lizzie whispered to me. "To get away from home and have an adventure!"

I must say that Lizzie is one of the bravest girls I have ever met. Or maybe because there are eight children in her family, she does not fear being overheard when she says such things.

"Will we see the *New Orleans*, Father?" Lizzie asked. "We do live near the Mississippi."

"It is expected to come through New Madrid sometime soon," Mr. Bryan said with a smile.

"Supper!" Mrs. Bryan called out the cabin door.

A swarm of children rushed to the well and plunged their hands in a bucket of water hanging there. There was much laughter and shouting as Lizzie's brothers and sisters jostled each other to wash their hands. Before too long, they all hurried past me into the house and shuffled and tripped over one another until they were seated.

All through supper, the children talked and gulped and chewed with their mouths wide open, in a perfect state of happiness, it appeared to me. Mr. and Mrs. Bryan made halfhearted attempts to quiet them. I could see that they were not hopeful, but they appeared not to be bothered at all.

Mama seemed a bit taken aback by the noisy nature of the meal, but I enjoyed it immensely. Only at the end of supper, when the children all leaped out of their chairs and raced to the yard to play again, did my heart feel squeezed in my chest. How lonely I will be when we return to our remote home in the wilderness!

Zoey

Mom and I were at Grandma Cope's house tonight. Since Thanksgiving, Mom has insisted on stopping over there every day to take Grandma's blood pressure. I can tell it's about to drive Grandma crazy, but there's no stopping Mom when she gets something in her head.

Right when we got there, Mom dropped a bomb. "Zoey," Mom said as I tried to chew through a hard oat bran muffin she insisted I eat, "I'm thinking about going on your field trip. The permission slip said they need more parent chaperones."

My mom? Chaperoning? No way! She might try to get the whole class to broaden their horizons by eating organic food and singing some old Beatles songs—or worse yet, "Kumbaya."

A hunk of muffin went down the wrong tube. I started choking and coughing. Mom jumped into action and performed a quick—and probably unnecessary—

Heimlich maneuver on me. The muffin chunk shot out onto the floor.

"We've got plenty of chaperones, Mom," I said when I could breathe. "A bunch of parents already volunteered and paid."

"Oh, what a shame!" Mom said. "I hate to say this, Zoey, but I don't want you to go on the trip to Reelfoot."

"What are you talking about, Mom? You've already paid for it. It's this coming Monday!" I stood up from the table.

"I can't help how I feel. I'm having a premonition, I think," she said. "The whole aura of this trip gives me a bad feeling."

"Nonsense, Marissa," Grandma Cope said. "It'll be good for her to see where she comes from—where *we* come from. I think she should go."

"You do?" I asked.

Grandma nodded. "Yes. That's near where I lived as a girl. I'm glad you're going."

"See?" I said to Mom. "I'm only going a couple hundred miles away, in the same state, to look at a lake."

"I could go as a chaperone. I certainly know a lot about Chickasaw Country," Grandma said. "Have you told your teacher that some of your family comes from West Tennessee?"

For just a second, I had a mental image of Jillian and me squeezed into a bus seat with Grandma Cope. And everyone looking at us. And asking questions. I felt my face flame with heat.

Mom was staring at Grandma and pumping away on the little ball that blows up the blood pressure cuff. "That's a great idea, Mother," she said. "I'll pay your way."

Grandma winced. "I think you can let that go now," she said, pointing to the tight cuff on her arm. "So, Zoey, where should I meet you on Monday morning?"

Suddenly, I felt like the top of my head was going to blow off. It's bad enough that my parents act all weird with each other; I don't want to deal with them—or Grandma—at school, too.

"I'm going, Mom. And you're not! And neither are you, Grandma! And that's it!" I shouted. "I don't want either one of you there, talking about our private life!" I saw Grandma's face fall. I ran out the door and threw myself into Mom's car before I started feeling guilty.

Mom came out a few minutes later. "You owe your grandmother an apology," she said. "And me, too."

I put on my headphones and turned up the volume. I think *they* owe *me* an apology.

December 12, Thursday

The chaperoning idea fell through (thank goodness!). Three of Mom's patients are due any minute now, she says, and she needs to be nearby. I've never been happier than I am right now that Mom is doing what she says is her "calling." And Grandma hasn't mentioned it again. Not that I've seen her.

Mom made a lot more money as a nurse, but she loves helping women who want to have their babies at home. Sometimes she makes me come along on her house calls because she doesn't want to leave me alone at night. It's gross! Why can't they go to a nice sterile hospital like normal people?

Grandma fusses about my attitude toward midwifery. She says Mom does important work and money isn't everything and I could learn something from her. "Pay attention, Zoey!" she told me once, like I might be tested on it someday!

Mom still feels there's a bad aura around the trip, but I convinced her I should go by telling her that half my term grade in social studies depends on the knowledge I acquire at Reelfoot. Some big words, along with the promise of an A in social studies, wiped out the bad karma, I guess, because she said, "Well, okay, but wear your seat belt on the bus the whole time, honey."

I conveniently neglected to remind Mom that school buses don't have seat belts, at least not here. And it's a good thing. She might start some grassroots campaign to have them installed. That's my mom for you.

Unfortunately, just when I got Mom settled down, Dad started acting paranoid about the trip! He said Mom called him at work earlier to discuss the aura that's had her so freaked out. He thought her concerns were "relevant." (His word, *not* mine!) I gave him the same speech about my grade for the semester, and even threw in some nonsense about getting into a good college and saving the world. He caved. I don't see what the big deal is. You'd think they'd both be glad to have a couple of days without me.

After school, I began organizing all the things I need for the trip. I don't care what Ms. Drummond says about modern conveniences—I need my cell phone and my iPod. If I hide them in my backpack, Ms. Drummond will be too busy examining the *flora* and the *fauna* to notice what I brought. At least, I hope she will.

I was just dozing off after midnight when I heard the craziest sound. I listened for a few minutes, hoping it would go away, but it didn't. Finally, I went into Mom's room. She was reading in bed.

"Do you hear that?" I asked.

Mom put her book down. "I heard it. I swear it sounds like a rooster crowing!"

"Well, why the heck is he doing that now?"

Mom laughed. That was nice. She doesn't laugh a lot like she used to. "Grandma Cope once told me about roosters crowing at night," she said, "something to do with the weather, I think."

I went back to my room. I heard a skittering from the corner and went over to look into my hamster's cage. The poor thing was going nuts trying to get out! He looked really wild-eyed. I stroked his back. "Calm down, Hamhock," I whispered.

I went back to bed, but that crazy rooster kept crowing and Hamhock kept racing. I'll have to ask Grandma Cope about it when I get back from my trip.

Prudence

14 December 1811

Kalopin appeared today. He stepped out of the woods as I was heading toward the barn. I stopped in my tracks.

"I came to warn you," Kalopin said. He looked quite serious, more so than I have ever known him to be.

I inched closer to where he stood near the edge of the forest, looking back toward the cabin to see if Mama was watching us.

"I fear Copiah's curse has begun," Kalopin said. "Soon there will be a great shaking of the earth. The river will fight itself within its own banks. You must leave."

"Where should we go? When?" My voice cracked. Again, I looked at the cabin. Mama was at the door now.

"Soon." Kalopin pointed east. "You must make your way to safety, toward where the sun rises, away from the big river."

"Prudence Charity! Come inside this moment!" Mama hollered.

"Do not wait for your father to return. There is no time. The land will turn in upon itself, crack open, and burn."

I admit that I believed him. Curse or not, nothing is strange to me these days. Restless energy fills the air, even at night. The animals are nervous and fidgety, pawing and snorting at nothing.

"Prudence!" Mama was agitated. "I said come inside now!"

King George brayed loudly in the field.

"Do not delay. It is time," Kalopin said, and turned to go.

I grabbed his arm. "Wait! What about you? Are you leaving?"

Mama was coming across the yard. I let go of Kalopin.

"I am taking my people to safety." Kalopin smiled, and then faded into the woods. One moment he was standing in front of me; the next he was gone.

"How long have you been talking to that savage?"

"Only a moment, Mama!" I shouted. "And he is not a savage! He came to warn us."

"Warn us? About what?"

"He says we must leave Chickasaw Country! He says that the ground will rumble soon and something about the river and—"

"Get control of yourself, daughter!" Mama pinched my arm.

I straightened my apron and my dress, cleared my

throat, and composed myself. Mama and I returned to the house.

I am still angry with her, but I do understand that she is terrified of the Indians. Each time I try to argue that there are some peaceful Indians, she reminds me of every raid we have ever heard about. She also tries to frighten me by reminding me how some Indians kidnap people and scalp them. But that is not the Chickasaw way.

Rain is coming. I smell it in the air. I will go to the barn soon and take care of the animals and get King George into the barn.

Should I try to talk to Mama later about Kalopin's warnings? He seemed very certain of this coming upheaval.

Zoey

December 16, Monday

It is the crack of dawn (really, it's eight a.m.) and we're on the road to Reelfoot. Slowly, surely, we are creeping down the highway, far away from school and our blubbering, waving parents. (You'd think we were leaving Nashville for a month, not two days!) We've already made it to West Tennessee.

I looked to the back of the bus where a couple of parent chaperones were sitting and was thankful that I'd been able to talk Mom and Grandma out of coming along.

Knowing we'd be at our campgrounds soon, I pulled out my makeup case and added some black mascara, blue eyeliner, green shadow, and some hot strawberry lip gloss.

"C'mon, Jillian," I said. Jillian put some makeup on, too, much to my relief. I was afraid she was going to go all boring on me.

"Are you sure it's not too much?" Jillian whispered to me.

"Don't worry, we look fabulous," I said back, but quietly. Robbie and Quentin were sitting in front of us. I didn't want them to hear us talking about ourselves.

Too late. Robbie turned around and looked at us with our mirrors in our hands. He elbowed Quentin, and he turned around, too. I tried to put the makeup away, but I dropped the mascara and the eye shadow. Jillian and I both bent down at the same time to pick them up and banged our heads.

"Ouch," we said together.

Quentin smirked. "Hey, Smith-Jones," he said. "Nice leather and fringe. Are you going totally *peoples* on us?"

I looked down at my outfit. It was rather . . . different looking, now that I think about it. But it was the only jacket I could find so early in the morning. Grandma Cope bought it for me last Christmas. "Well, you know me," I said, aiming for a light tone. "Anything for extra credit."

Robbie smiled. I decided I'd wear a burlap sack to see that smile again. "Hey, you got any gum?" Robbie interrupted my thoughts. He looked right at me with his sparkly brown eyes.

"Yes," I said, mesmerized.

Robbie was still smiling, not smirking.

"Well, can I have some?" he asked.

"Some what?"

"Some gum?" This time he laughed. He might have been smirking a little, too. Dang it all.

"Oh, sure. Hang on." I threw my makeup into my purse and then dug around in the front pocket of my backpack.

"We're not supposed to chew gum," Jillian said. "Remember what Mr. Capers said before we got on the bus?"

"He always says that," I pointed out.

Quentin cleared his throat and pretended to hack up a big old loogie. *"Now lookit!"* he said in a perfect imitation of Mr. Capers. *"You brats gum up my bus, and you'll spend tonight scraping!"*

Robbie and I busted up. After a few seconds, Jillian did, too, which was good. She needs to lighten up. I looked across the aisle, though, and Mike MacPherson was frowning.

I found the gum and handed Robbie and Quentin each a piece. Jillian stuck her hand out, so I gave her one, and I tossed a piece over to Mike, too. Then I popped a piece in my mouth and tried to chew without smacking my lips too loudly. Not that it mattered. Robbie and Quentin immediately turned around and put their headphones on. So much for conversation.

Just as I was settling in with Jillian for a good game of hangman, Mike leaned across the aisle.

"You want to see this book about Reelfoot Lake?" he asked. In his hand was an old book. He pushed his glasses up on his nose with the other hand. Then he turned red.

"Now, why would I want to do that?" I said, glancing ahead of me to see if Robbie and Quentin were paying any attention. "We're going to *see* Reelfoot Lake, aren't we?"

Mike's face fell. I felt bad, but he is always trying to get my attention. I sighed. "Okay, let me see it."

Mike handed the book over. It was one of those dense old history books with a dirt-brown cover, like I've seen at Grandma Cope's house. I opened it and the print was so tiny I could barely make out the words. I brought the book up to my nose. A wet, musty smell made me sneeze. I wiped the wet spots off the pages with my sleeve and began reading.

> **The legend of Reelfoot is one that has never died. Since the New Madrid Earthquakes, a number of other strange legends have sprung up over the years among those citizens who claim that their ancestors lived through the disaster.**

A delicious little shiver made its way down my spine.

"Look at the sky!" Jillian said.

I looked out the window. The sky had darkened to that eerie green-black color we always see before bad storms or even tornadoes. A crash of thunder drowned out the laughter and talking on the bus. Ms. Drummond was leaning forward in her seat, talking to Mr. Capers. She waved her hands toward the front window of the bus a few times, pointing at the dark sky.

"I'll bet we're going to turn around," Jillian said.

"I hope not!" I said. "I don't want to go home." And

I didn't. Suddenly, more than anything, I wanted to see Reelfoot Lake—and Chickasaw Country.

The bus slowed and then pulled to a stop under a highway overpass. Everyone got quiet when Mr. Capers stood up.

"I'm getting off this bus, lady!" he said to Ms. Drummond. "And I suggest you get off, too, and get these brats into a ditch. It's not safe here—I see a twister up ahead!" He opened the door of the bus and jumped down. I looked out my window and saw him run toward the drainage ditch beside the highway.

"A twister?" I said to Jillian. All around us, everyone began shouting and shoving to get to the front of the bus.

"Please stay calm!" Ms. Drummond shouted above the clamor. "Leave everything and get off the bus immediately!" She jumped down the front steps, and one of the chaperoning dads opened the emergency exit and started helping kids out that way.

My heart thundered in my chest. I clutched Mike's old book with one hand, and with the other I reached into my pocket and grabbed the crystal Mom had insisted I bring. Its cool, smooth surface did not make me feel any better. I felt worse, really, because now I was homesick for Mom and Dad. What were they going to say about this?

Someone was tugging me toward the emergency exit. It was Mike. "Wait! My backpack!" I yelled, and turned around.

"Forget it!" Jillian said. "Come on!"

"But my iPod's in there! And my cell phone. I have to get them or Dad will kill me," I said. "I'll meet you outside."

I tried to push my way back down the aisle but got nowhere, so I climbed over the seat backs until I reached my seat. I found my backpack on the floor of the bus, and I threw Mike's old book into it. I yanked on my jacket.

When I turned around, the bus was empty and quiet. I ran up the aisle and practically fell down the steps of the bus.

Booming thunder that cracked in my ears was followed immediately by zigzagging lightning that lit up the completely black sky. Without the lightning, I couldn't see an inch in front of me.

"Jillian! Where are you?" I hollered into the wind. It was so strong it pushed me back against the bus.

"We're under the bridge! Under the overpass! Head to your right," I heard Jillian say, her voice faint. The wind was fierce, and pounding rain exploded out of nowhere. Within seconds, there was rushing water on the highway. Flash flood!

A blinding light illuminated the highway for a second, but then darkness fell again. I headed to my right and tripped, falling into the drainage ditch. The rushing water grabbed me and swept me farther away from everyone. Another blinding flash, and then agonizing pain in my leg. Then nothing.

Prudence

It has rained all day. Late this afternoon I stood at the door of our cabin looking out into the dreary wet yard. I had a quilt wrapped around my shoulders, but it did not warm me or make me feel any less damp. There was a queer smell in the air, like rotting eggs, but even that could not force me inside the cheerless cabin.

I could not get Kalopin and his warnings off my mind, try though I did. Every strange sound made me jump. I had been longing to see him, but now I wish he had not come!

Would that something exciting might happen!

Sometimes I believe that my life is over, but I have not yet begun to live! All I do all the livelong day is chores, and for what? To get up and do them all over again. Feed the animals, chop the wood, collect the kindling, help cook, mend our clothes, and on and on. Mama is sad or fretful most of the time, dear Papa is gone most of the time, and I am stuck here in this

Godforsaken place all of the time! Alone and with no one to talk to besides my mother!

"Prudence, dear, close the door, please, and come inside," Mama called.

"Mama, I cannot bear to sit in the dark another moment," I said a mite snappishly. I bit my tongue the moment the words left my mouth, knowing I had probably hurt her. There was a long silence behind me. I turned to look. Mama sat with her head down and her shoulders drooping.

"I am so sorry," I said, closing the door. "But I wish there were someone to talk to. It is so tedious to not be able to go outside or see folks," I said, and then bit my tongue again. "Not that I do not enjoy talking with you, Mama."

To my surprise, Mama laughed. "I understand your feelings. I was once a young girl, too," she said, and picked up her knitting needles.

"What did you do with yourself on days like this?" I asked.

"I made myself busy with sewing and mending."

"That is what I thought you would say," I said. I sighed deeply and opened the door again.

Outside, thunder cracked and lightning flashed, brightening up the yard around the cabin for a split second.

Something was falling through the trees.

I closed my eyes, shook my head, and looked again. The yard was dark. It had to have been a falling branch,

I surmised, but it surely was a large one. That thought cheered me. A large branch, right by the cabin, would make for easy firewood. No chopping and toting it a half mile home.

Tonight, after the rain stopped, I watched the two-tailed comet and made a wish. For a friend. How I long for a friend!

Zoey

December 16, Monday (continued)

I tried to open my eyes, but they felt gummy and scratchy. My wet hair rested like a heavy quilt across my face. Every bone in my body ached. I lay another moment, trying to remember what had happened. It was very dark, and I wondered if I'd slept all day.

After a few fuzzy minutes, I remembered the storm. I reached down and felt my thigh. My leather pants had a hole in them, and I could feel a burning sensation from the top of my leg to my ankle. I had been struck by lightning! Mom would have a fit.

My head felt woozy, and I felt so stiff and creaky, it was difficult to sit up. Once I got myself upright, I leaned against a tree and looked around. Not that I could see much. It was dark like I've never seen before, with the clouds covering the moon.

After I'd been sitting there a minute or two, the moon broke through the clouds, and I eased my way to my feet, holding on to the big tree for support, and took stock of my situation. In front of me, through a dim mist, I could see a ramshackle barn. A few paces away from that was another structure that looked similar to the barn, but more like a cabin. A huge pile of firewood, as tall as the cabin itself, leaned against the wall.

There was no sign of the bus. Or the highway, either, for that matter. The barn was closer. I decided to make a run for it. It had to be warmer and drier in the barn than outside.

I edged away from the tree and stood without its support for a moment. I felt dizzy again, and my leg hurt. I put my hand to my head and brushed the damp hair out of my eyes, then took a deep breath. I didn't know the extent of my injuries from the lightning strike, but I'd watched enough *General Hospital* in my life to figure out that I might have been unconscious for a while.

"I'll bet I'm in shock," I said aloud. My voice sounded weak. "Too bad cute Dr. Baxter from *General Hospital* isn't around to check me over. But I'll bet he'd tell me to get warm and get help."

I hitched my backpack up onto my shoulders. Amazing, really, that I hadn't lost it. As I began to walk toward the barn, another downpour began. Careful not to fall, and worrying over the state of my electronics, I hurried, slipping and sliding through the mud until I reached the door of the barn.

Just inside, I stopped and pulled my cell phone out of my backpack. I turned it on. Nothing. *Probably wet, like me,* I thought, and put the phone back in my backpack.

My leather jeans and jacket were soaked, too. "Mom's going to be so mad when she sees the condition of this outfit," I said to myself, looking down at my ruined clothes. Suddenly I felt so scared that I almost started bawling. My face got hot and my heart was galloping around in my chest.

Where was I? We had almost reached Reelfoot when the storm blew up. I wondered if it would take a long time for Ms. Drummond and Mr. Capers to find me. I wondered if anyone else was lost. I breathed in and out, little fast puffs, like I had heard Mom instruct her patients to do. That made me feel more lightheaded, until I remembered that for calming down, I needed deep, slow "cleansing" breaths, as Mom called them. Another wave of dizziness sent me spilling to the ground.

A slight rocking motion beneath me lulled me at first, but as it grew stronger, and the walls of the barn began creaking around me, I bolted upright.

"Earthquake!" I whispered to myself. I clambered up and ran out of the barn. I could feel the ground rolling beneath my feet.

A nasty, rotten-egg smell was seeping out of the ground. I put my hand over my nose, but there was no escaping it.

Lightning flashed. I wondered if there were people in the cabin, and began making my way toward it. Just as

I reached for the door, it opened, and I stared into the scared face of a girl about my own age. She was holding an old-fashioned lantern.

"Earthquake!" was all I could think to say to her.

We stood for a second looking at each other before the ground bucked beneath us, throwing us to our knees. The girl dropped the lantern and broke it, but the flame went out, which was a blessing. We had enough on our hands without dealing with a fire, too.

I heard dishes and other glassware crashing to the cabin floor, and stones were tumbling from the fireplace behind her. I felt like my heart was pounding as loudly as the thunder.

The floor beneath us jerked and jolted like the Greezed Lightnin' at Kentucky Kingdom, making it difficult to stand.

"Prudence! Prudence, help me," a weak voice called from behind a curtain.

"I am coming, Mama!" The girl, Prudence, began crawling toward the curtained area. She was doing her best, but not making much headway.

I began crawling toward Prudence as more stones fell from the fireplace. The log walls on both sides of the chimney were shifting and creaking.

Behind the curtain, a woman struggled to sit upright. The floor buckled and sent her tumbling off the bed. She screamed as she hit the floor, clutching her huge belly.

"We have to get out of the house now," I said to the

girl and her mother, which seemed like a bit of an understatement, considering the circumstances.

"Oh no!" the woman whispered, looking at me. "Indians!"

"What?" I asked. "Where?" I looked around. What was she talking about?

"Mama, we will help you. We need to get outside before you get hurt." Prudence sounded much calmer than I felt.

"I fear I cannot walk," the woman whispered.

I looked around. "The quilt. Let's put your mom on the quilt and we can carry her out." When Prudence just stood there, I shouted at her. "We need to hurry!"

Prudence looked at me and nodded. She pulled the quilt off the bed. "Mama, lie on this," she commanded.

"No, I cannot. I am afraid! I do not want to do anything that might harm the baby," the woman protested with a whimper.

"If we don't get you out of here, the house is going to crash down around our heads," I said as I helped the girl straighten the quilt out on the floor.

The gross smell made me want to gag.

The woman crawled to the quilt, sat down, leaned back, and then rolled onto her side. When there was a momentary pause in the bucking of the floor, Prudence and I stood up.

"On my count," I said, "then lift. One, two, lift!" I lifted my two sides of the quilt at the same time

Prudence did. Despite her huge belly, the woman wasn't all that heavy.

We stepped with care around the household items littering the floor. It was hard going, but we made our way to the front door of the cabin, which was open and dangling, and hurried out into the frigid night air.

When we were far enough away from the cabin to escape falling objects, we settled the woman on the ground. She moaned and began to shiver with the cold. Around us, fissures opened in the ground and repulsive fumes spewed out.

"We need more blankets and clothes," Prudence said to me. "We will freeze if we don't cover up."

The screech of splintering trees and the crash of falling branches made me jump. "Shouldn't we wait until things calm down?" I said.

Prudence wrapped the edge of the quilt around her mother. "I do not know how long this will last. It is bitter tonight. But I fear we will be harmed if we go back into the cabin."

The woman whimpered. Prudence's teeth chattered.

Prudence looked at her mother and then at me. She walked a few feet away from the woman. I followed her. "We need food. And our bedding. And we need to get some of the coals from the fireplace," she continued, grabbing my arm.

"Why?" Coals? For what?

"Because we will need heat, and a way to light a lamp later, if all of the lamps are not broken," Prudence said, as if this made perfect sense. Where were all their flashlights? "Without heat, we might all fall ill. Mama is shaking in an awful way!"

I nodded. Food and blankets sounded good to me, and heat would be even better. I was shivering, too.

Without warning, a sob burst from the girl, but she stopped herself from crying after only a second. "I must keep Mama safe! I promised Papa I would take care of her."

I wished my mom was with me. I'd try to keep her safe, too. Thinking about Mom made me feel like crying, but I didn't have that luxury.

"What should I put the coals in?" I asked Prudence.

"Put them in the bucket by the chimney. Put ashes in the bottom first so the coals won't burn through."

Prudence's instructions sounded so strange to me, but there was no time to think. The ground rolled beneath us. We clutched each other to keep from falling down.

"It might be too dangerous to go in there now. Perhaps we should wait," Prudence said.

"What if things get worse?" I asked. "One of us has to do it. You stay here with your mom. I'll go." I took off my backpack and gave it to her. During a lull in the tremors, I ran toward the cabin, stumbling and tripping as I went.

"Be careful," the girl shouted over her shoulder as she made her way to her mother. I noticed she was holding my backpack away from her and looking at it in a weird way.

I couldn't believe I was going into that rickety cabin, but I did. I wondered how Jillian and the rest of my class were doing and where they were. I hoped they were in a safer place than I had managed to find. I planned to look for them as soon as things settled down. That thought made me feel stronger. I maneuvered my way across the uneven floor to get the blankets we needed.

Inside, I began wheezing immediately from the horrific stench that had invaded the cabin. I gagged. I had smelled that odor before. The night Mom and I were at Mambo Taco!

I looked around, trying to see where things might be.

Another boom of thunder, and the ground swayed. I dropped to the floor and crouched down to wait for the shaking to subside; then I grabbed the quilts and pallets from the floor and threw them out the door of the cabin. Another hard tremor shook the house. I fell hard, scraping my knees. Tears sprang to my eyes. I wanted to get out of there! I wanted to be anywhere but in that cabin!

I stepped outside, but then I remembered the coals. I hurried back toward the fireplace, where the embers still burned. The ash bucket sat beside the fireplace with a shovel in it. What kind of house was this? No electricity? An ash bucket? This place looked so different from any house I'd ever seen.

I'd never even lit a fire before, but I began shoveling the hot coals into the bucket, the way I used to shovel sand into my bucket at the beach, being careful not to burn my hands.

Through the open door, I could see lightning flashing and made out Prudence's silhouette as she came to gather up the quilts. Her long white nightgown was soaked, and I knew that if we didn't get warm soon, we would all start going into shock from the cold. I'd seen that happen on an episode of *General Hospital*.

By the time I got outside, the girl was huddled with her mother across the yard. I made my way to them as fast as I could, carrying the bucket with the hot coals. The sounds of cows bawling and chickens squawking in the barn made me wince. I knew they had to be scared. I was! Worse than that were Prudence's whimpers and her mother's moans.

All around us, branches cracked off tree trunks and crashed to the ground. Trees were splitting in half vertically, and some were sheared close to the ground, as if an invisible buzz saw was making its way around the area. I looked to see the girl covering her mother's body with her own.

Suddenly, the ground burst open beside me and sand and water spewed up out of it. Small rocks pelted my skin. I screamed as the hot rocks nicked and burned my hands. The girl and the woman were screaming, too. I put my arms over my head and rolled into a ball.

As the ground stopped rolling and the noise diminished somewhat, I heard the thumps and thuds of several pieces of the chimney hitting the ground. Vapor seeped out of the earth. I hurried to where the ash bucket had fallen over and pushed some of the hot coals back into it, singeing my fingers. Then I rose and made my way to Prudence and her mother.

The three of us huddled together, watching the world go to pieces around us. A hard tremor, though not as violent as some before, shook the earth beneath us. The cabin hitched back and forth and then began to fall in on itself. Prudence started to cry.

Prudence

There has been a horrible earthquake that shows no signs of ceasing, just as Kalopin warned. And a most unusual occurrence! I must record every detail so that I forget nothing.

Just as the tremors began, early in the hours before dawn, I awoke. I went to the door of our cabin and flung it open to see what was happening outside. There, standing on our stoop, was a stranger. I could not tell at first if this person was a man or woman, boy or girl, because of the darkness. Within a few moments, the earthquake began in earnest, and Mama called out to me.

From the firelight inside the cabin, I determined the stranger to be a girl about my own age, an Indian, from the looks of her dress. Paint was smeared on her face. Her leathers were soaked but looked of good quality.

We spent the next few hours huddling in the open

with our quilts, which the girl retrieved from the cabin for us at great risk to herself. Around dawn, the world quieted and we could talk.

"You speak English," I said to the girl.

"Of course!" she answered. "What else would I speak?"

"Are you not an Indian?" I asked. "The Chickasaw chief is my friend." I wondered if she knew Kalopin.

The girl seemed quite taken aback by this observation, but she does appear to be an Indian. I looked over at Mama, who slept restlessly in her quilt on the ground.

"I'm not an Indian!" she said. "My Grandma Cope is part Chickasaw and part Choctaw, but I'm just an eensy bit of any of that." The girl took a deep breath. "And why do you care, anyway?"

"Mama is scared of Indians," I said. "And if your grandmother is an Indian, then you are Indian, too." I looked at her closely. Most certainly, her hair was straight and dark, like Kalopin's, and her eyes were dark, almost black. Her high cheekbones reminded me of Kalopin's as well.

"Stop saying that," she said. "I'm nowhere near full-blooded. My dad's family is probably from England or somewhere."

"What is your name?" I asked.

"Zoey," she said.

A most unusual name. I like it.

"My name is Prudence Charity," I told her.

"That's a long name," Zoey said. "How about I call you Pru?"

I smiled. Pru. Sometimes Papa calls me that. I wish he were here to help us. I hope he has survived and comes home to us soon.

"I'm so hungry I could eat a horse," Zoey said. "Or a mule!" She laughed at that, seeming to find it quite funny.

I looked over at the remains of the barn. Our other animals appeared to have run off, but King George remained. "I do not think I could eat a mule," I said. The thought of having to eat my friend King George made me sick.

Zoey looked over at King George, too. "Sorry," she said, "I didn't *really* mean it! I was only kidding around, Pru."

"We do have venison and apples," I said. "In the cellar. We will have to go and find some food today."

"What's venison?" Zoey asked.

That was a strange question coming from an Indian, I thought. Zoey must have been addled from the earthquake. "Deer meat," I told her. "Venison is deer meat."

"No way am I eating deer!" Zoey cried, backing away from me. "I'll just have apples. They're *regular* apples, aren't they?" she asked.

"Of course," I said. I felt I needed to reassure her, but I did not know why. "We should get some food out of the cabin soon. We must eat."

"Hey, do you have a phone? Mine seems to be

dead," Zoey said. "I need to call my parents. Or nine-one-one, maybe. I'd say this definitely qualifies as an emergency."

What is a "phone"? I wondered. I looked at my new friend. Not much of what she said made sense. I wondered if Zoey might be one of those white children captured by Indians as a child. She is not like any of the girls I know from Knoxville, or even New Madrid, nor is she as Indian as Kalopin. But the streaks of black, blue, green, and red running down Zoey's face were surely the remnants of war paint. I had seen the same chamois leggings and fringed jacket on an Indian at the general store in New Madrid, though many of the Indians now wear regular britches and shirts.

Maybe if Kalopin comes back soon, he can observe Zoey and tell me if he knows her or has heard of her. Until then, though, I am not at all certain what I should do.

I wondered if I should tell Mama that Zoey was an Indian captive. Surely she would want to help Zoey. Mama has never turned away a body in need.

I ignored her question. "Do you know a mingo they call Reelfoot?" I used the name the whites use for Kalopin, hoping Zoey might recognize it.

"What's a mingo?" Zoey asked.

"A mingo. A chief. Do you know Reelfoot?"

Zoey seemed quite exasperated with me at this question. "I told you! Grandma Cope is Choctaw and Chickasaw, but I'm Americana mishmash," she said. "I have heard of Reelfoot, though. That's why I'm here! I came on a field trip with my class to see the lake."

I felt as if lightning had struck me! "Reelfoot is not a lake! He is a young Indian chief," I whispered.

"You mean he *was* a young chief," Zoey said. "Reelfoot has been dead and gone for years and years."

I do not understand much of what Zoey says. But I will not believe that Kalopin is dead!

Zoey

December 16 (continued)

After things calmed down a bit, Pru huddled near her mother, talking in a low tone. She had gone behind a tree earlier and changed her clothes. She'd offered me some clothes, but I wasn't ready to get too comfortable. Ms. Drummond might show up any minute.

Even though Pru had no makeup on and wore some seriously weird clothes—as in a long granny dress and an apron—she looked pretty. A shaft of moonlight broke through the clouds and shone on her hair, which is a reddish color with golden strands running through the two heavy braids. Her eyes are blue.

While she and her mother were busy, I got up and walked toward what was left of the barn. I stopped and pulled my cell phone out of my backpack. I pressed the On button. It beeped at me this time! Apparently, it had not been damaged by the lightning and the water.

"Yahoo!" I whispered. My heart beat a little faster. I knew I should call my parents, but I didn't want to worry them if my teacher was nearby. I'd try to call one of my friends first and get Ms. Drummond on the phone. I knew Jillian didn't have her cell with her, since she always follows the rules, so I pressed the numbers for Mike's and put the phone to my ear.

Nothing. It had clicked off. No signal. I pressed On again. It searched and searched for a signal and then off it went. I turned it on again, feeling a little panicky. *Should I dial 911?* I wondered. Maybe I should wait until I talked to Pru. Surely she had a cell phone or could take me to a telephone.

Whinny-ah-haw!

I jumped. There was that mule again. I hadn't seen him.

"How far out in the boonies am I?" I asked the animal.

Ah-haw! he brayed back, loudly, making me jump again.

I sat down on a log to consider my situation. I didn't know where I was, and I didn't know where my friends and Ms. Drummond were. My only hope for rescue was this Pru girl, who was so into history that she had offered me a chunk of dried-up deer meat to eat. Gross.

The moon appeared for a moment, and I could see their destroyed house now. I didn't know anyone lived in the state park. I thought about looking for the visitors' center or a gift shop that must be around somewhere, but I still felt a little woozy, and I didn't want to get more lost than I was already.

Maybe Ms. Drummond will come along soon.

Someone has to be looking for me. Mom and Dad always tell me that if I get lost, I should stay in one place and let help find me. Otherwise, everyone just wanders around, which is no help at all.

My head hurt, and I felt drowsy. I wasn't scared. Not yet. If someone didn't find me soon, I decided, then I'd get scared. I closed my eyes and drifted off to sleep.

"Zoey? Zoey?" Prudence's voice cut through my dreamless fog and I came awake. She looked worried. There was a big wrinkle between her eyes, and she was twisting her apron in her hands.

"There you are. I hoped you had not run away from us," she said, her voice relieved.

"Run where?" I shot back. I felt bad when I saw the stricken look on Pru's face.

"To return to the Indians?" Prudence asked.

"What *Indians*? I just want to find my friends and my teacher," I said. "I know they're around here somewhere."

"Yes, it has been a long time since you have seen them, I suppose," Prudence said.

"I think I'm lost." Suddenly I felt scared just saying the words. "Don't you think they're looking for me by now?"

"Do not worry. You are with us, Zoey. Perhaps we can find your family." Prudence seemed to be examining my pants and my braids. "If you are not an Indian, were you kidnapped by Indians? Mama has told me that happens."

"What are you talking about?" I shook my head. "Listen, Pru, I tried to call my friend Mike, but my cell phone is on the fritz," I said, worried. How long had I been lost, and no one had found me yet? My heart rate picked up speed. "Do you have your cell phone? Or can you take me to a land line?"

Pru looked confused. Again.

"What is this *cell phone* you speak of?" Pru said. "I'm sorry, but I do not think we have one."

"What am I supposed to do, then?" I asked. I sounded whiny, which made me mad at myself. I only sound whiny when I'm scared, and I hate admitting that I'm scared.

"I have been talking with Mama. I think we should try to travel to the fort," Pru said. "But we will wait for Papa. When Papa returns, he will know what to do."

"How long until he returns?"

Prudence looked dismayed for a second. "Surely by Christmas. He promised he would be home no later than that."

"Christmas! I can't wait until then! I've got to get home by tomorrow night or Mom will have a fit!"

"I am most sorry," Prudence said.

"I'm most sorry, too," I said back.

Pru had that worried look on her face again. "Zoey, I must tell you something."

"Shoot," I said.

Prudence took a deep breath. "I must properly introduce you to Mama, but I must tell you that you have to do as I say. Mama fears the Indian savages, as she calls them, with all her being, and if she thinks you are in any way related to them, she will be too frightened to let you remain with us."

"What do you mean 'Indian savages'? Don't you know that most Native Americans would find that offensive?"

Prudence looked confused. "I am not sure what you mean. . . ."

"You can't say savages! And Native Americans don't like to be called Indians! At least, I don't *think* they do." It struck me then that I've never asked Grandma Cope what she prefers to be called. I know what I'd pick—nothing at all.

Prudence shook her head. "Please listen. I believe that you do not remember who you are or where you are from, and that is understandable, since you sustained an injury in the storm. Perhaps it knocked you senseless."

"Hey!" I said. "I'm not—"

"I must tell my mother that you are a white girl who was an Indian captive. You must make her believe this to be true, or we cannot help you."

Although I was certain that Pru must have sustained an injury herself, the words "help you" convinced me to go along. "Okay, Pru, whatever you say. All I know is that I'm freezing, and I need to find a way to contact my parents and get home." I grabbed my backpack and limped over to where Pru's mother was sitting.

She had her hair pinned up in a tight bun, and was wearing the same kind of old-time dress as Pru.

"Mama, this is the girl I told you about who helped us get out of the house safely. Her name is Zoey," Pru said to her mother. "Zoey, this is my mother, Mrs. Grace Keeler."

"Hey, Mrs. Keeler," I said.

Mrs. Keeler stared at me with a weird scowl on her face. Her look clearly said she was suspicious of me. I couldn't blame her. Who was going to believe I'd been an Indian captive? That stuff only happens in the movies! After a moment, she spoke.

"Who is this girl?" she asked Pru.

"She is a girl who was taken captive by the Indians in a raid a long time ago. She escaped and made her way here."

"Her presence here unnerves me, Prudence."

I blushed. Mrs. Keeler spoke as if I wasn't right there in front of them listening.

"Mama, I believe Zoey is harmless."

"But you do not know that for certain, do you?"

Pru was quiet for a moment. "Mama, you know dear Papa would not turn Zoey away."

"Your papa is not here."

"It will be all right, Mama," she answered. "Maybe Zoey will be a help to us."

In answer, Mrs. Keeler turned her face from us and pulled the covers around her shoulders.

"She is hurt, Mama. I think we should help her."

Mrs. Keeler turned back to look at us. "You may stay with us until we can travel to the fort," she said. She looked tired. She closed her eyes.

"I appreciate it," I said, using my best talking-to-strange-adults voice. Pru's mother didn't answer me. She'd fallen asleep. Or she was acting like it.

"I still don't know where I am," I told Pru.

"Why, you are in Tennessee, in Chickasaw Country."

"Oh, I get it!" I said. "You must be one of those tour-guide girls." That was the only explanation for the outfit Prudence wore. She looked like the girls I saw working in Colonial Williamsburg when my parents dragged me there on vacation a couple of years ago.

"What do you mean?" Pru asked.

"You know, a tour guide who takes people around and tells them fun facts about old stuff." I looked around. "Is this near the visitors' center? Have you seen any of the other kids or Ms. Drummond or that foul Mr. Capers?"

Prudence shook her head. I continued to look around. This place was authentic looking, better than most other historical places I'd been to over the years. No obvious modern conveniences. The yard around the remains of the cabin was bare of grass, and there was a gigantic woodpile. That was about it. I couldn't get over how realistic this place looked. I just know that when I tell Mom and Dad about this, they'll want to drag me back for a tour.

"I really need a phone, Pru," I said.

"I do not understand," she said.

"A phone!" I shouted at Prudence. I was feeling a little frayed. "What, are you living in the Dark Ages?"

"No!" Prudence shocked me by shouting back. "The Dark Ages were hundreds of years ago. This is 1811!"

Prudence and I stared at one another.

I gulped. Hard. "Did you say 1811?"

"Of course. It is December sixteenth and it is 1811."

"You're kidding, right?" I said.

Pru took a deep breath. "I can assure you that it *is* 1811." Prudence seemed completely convinced that what she was saying was the honest truth.

I thought for a moment. Maybe I was on one of those practical-joke shows, or reality TV.

Not caring how silly I seemed to Prudence, I looked around for a hidden camera. But there was no sign of anything that looked like video equipment.

I turned to Pru, who was staring at me like I was some kind of an alien. "Who's the president?" I asked.

"Why, it is Mr. James Madison. Everyone knows that!"

"No, it's not!" My voice cracked. "Madison was the president like two hundred years ago!"

Pru's eyes grew so round, I thought they might pop out of her head. I felt like my eyes might pop out, too, and my face was all hot. "You've got to quit kidding around with me like this!"

"Zoey, I am very confused by what you say. Mr. Madison is our president, the fourth president, after Mr. Washington, Mr. Adams, and Mr. Jefferson. It is 1811, and Mr. Madison was inaugurated in 1809." Pru had lost her astounded look. It had been replaced by an assurance that made me wonder.

"Look, Pru, James Madison is *not* the president! We've had bunches of presidents since him!"

Pru swept a hand across her forehead, brushing her hair back. "What are you saying, Zoey?"

"I'm saying stop it! I don't know who put you up to this, but it is not 1811! There are fifty states and—"

"Fifty states?" Pru whispered. Then she shook her head hard, as if to clear it of such a crazy notion. I knew exactly how she was feeling.

"Zoey, our United States has had seventeen states since Ohio joined the union in 1803." Pru now looked very sure of herself again.

I shook my head and put my hands over my ears. I didn't want to play this game anymore. I wanted to go home and have hot cocoa with Grandma Cope while Mom and Dad went to the symphony. Then I wanted to go to sleep in my own comfortable bed, with central air and heat. It was cold outside—too cold.

"Zoey, rest now. Surely you are tired from your journey."

"Rest? Are you crazy? I can't sleep! Where's the bus? Where are Ms. Drummond and my friends? They're probably going nuts and calling the police, wondering what happened to me!"

"Girls, please!" Mrs. Keeler said from where she lay.

Pru stood and motioned me away from her mother.

I didn't want to leave the fire, but I followed her anyway.

I looked up at the comet, still visible in the dawn sky. It was the same comet I'd been watching for months back home.

When Pru saw where I was looking, she said, "The Indians say the comet is an omen. I have been watching it since March."

"Me too," I said. "On the news, all the scientists said this comet wasn't supposed to come back for a long time. They said it first appeared . . ." I backed up and sat down hard on the ground. "In 1811."

Prudence

Last night, Zoey finally ceased arguing with me about the year, I am happy to say, but she looked quite peaked when I helped her fix her pallet by the fire.

"Tell me again what year it is," she insisted.

I told her, many times. "It is 1811. James Madison is the president. There are seventeen states in the union. I live in Chickasaw Country in West Tennessee."

Zoey paced up and down, which upset Mama to no end because she was trying to sleep.

"Pru," Zoey said, "it can't be 1811."

"Please try to rest," I said. "I truly believe that you might be somewhat addled by what has happened to you." This only seemed to incite her more.

"I am not crazy!" she said. "I left Nashville on a bus yesterday, on an overnight field trip with my social studies class to see Reelfoot Lake. I know the lake was formed sometime in 1812, and now you're telling me it's 1811! I have to figure this out!"

"This is Chickasaw Country, and it is 1811, and there is no lake called Reelfoot Lake," I insisted, just as forcefully.

Zoey went to her pallet and wrapped herself in her blanket. Her face looked pinched and drawn, and her hands shook. "I have to figure this out," she muttered to herself, over and over.

Eventually, she slept. I lifted up a prayer that she would find peace and healing in her sleep, since I do not know how to help her figure out what is troubling her.

In the morning, Mama looked at the hole in Zoey's britches and the burn on her leg. "Prudence, we should try to find the salve for her burn," she said.

"Yes, Mama." I walked over to the cabin. In a few moments, I returned to Mama and Zoey.

"Take off your britches and put this salve on your wound," I said to Zoey.

She took the little jar I had given her. When she sniffed the contents, she nearly gagged. "That smells like roadkill! Nothing that smells that bad can be any good for your body," she said, and put the jar of salve down on a log.

Mama harrumphed at that. "It will not do any good in there," she said. Mama turned to me. "Your papa said he would move us to the fort at Christmastime. I think we should begin preparations to move now. And if Papa does not return as he promised, we will hitch that old mule to the wagon and take ourselves there." She had that hard, angry look on her face that scares me.

Zoey moved closer to me and Mama. "Isn't there any place closer we can go for help? Like a hospital?"

"Zoey," I said. This time my voice was sharp. I knew my new friend could hear the warning in my tone because her mouth clapped shut. "This is Obion, in the middle of Chickasaw Country. The closest place we can go for assistance is the fort across the river."

"Did you say Obion County?" Zoey asked me. There was a note of alarm in her voice. Mama heard it, too, because she looked up at Zoey.

Zoey motioned for me to walk with her, out of Mama's earshot. "You said Obion County, right?" she whispered.

"Well, not yet a county, but yes, Obion, in West Tennessee. I told you all of this last night. Why?"

"Pru, what day is it?" Zoey asked. Her voice shook. She looked like she might cry.

"It is the seventeenth day of December in . . ."

"Yes, I know, 1811. Right?" Zoey said.

"Yes, as I told you last night. And which you refused to believe, which is beyond my understanding. Why do you continue to ask?" I said. Zoey looked so fearful, I was beginning to feel afraid.

Zoey took a deep breath and lowered herself to the hard ground. She grabbed my arm most forcefully and would not let go. "We've got to get out of here. We've got to get help, Pru."

"Mama will be all right. We have managed on our own for some time now. I am sure we will make it through this time." I tried to shake Zoey's hand off my arm, but she held on. "And Papa will be home any day now, and no later than Christmas. He promised!" Saying that almost made me weep. I wanted my papa to return right away!

"It's not only about your mother, Pru. This place, this time." Zoey's voice had risen considerably, and Mama looked over at us. Zoey took another deep breath. "This whole area will disappear soon. We've got to leave now."

"I do not understand what you are saying, Zoey," I said. Mama was looking at Zoey as if she were a bear right in the middle of our yard. Or a ghost.

"I'm saying that this whole area of Tennessee is about to be hit by some of the biggest earthquakes ever—eight point eight on the Richter scale! We read about them in school," Zoey said. "Yesterday was just the beginning. These earthquakes are going to go on for months and the river will run backward and the whole place is going to flood! We've got to leave now."

"Richter scale? What's that? More earthquakes? A flood? Here?"

"Yes, in Obion County. We've got to find a way to get out of here!"

"I do not understand," I said again. "Why should we believe you?"

Zoey stood for a moment, lost in thought. Then she snapped her fingers. "Mike's book!" she said. She grabbed her pack, reached inside it, and pulled out a brown book. She opened it to the middle and read aloud:

> Earthquakes struck the western portion of Tennessee and the eastern area of what was then known as the Louisiana Territory in the winter of 1811. The earthquakes continued, unabated, for almost three months. The force of the quakes caused the Mississippi River to surge from its banks, forming Reelfoot Lake and drowning many people in its path.

Zoey turned to the front of the book. She began to speak, but then she looked at Mama and motioned for me to come closer. *Published 1925* was printed on the front page. I sucked in my breath. How could that be?

Zoey

December 17, 1811 (???!!!)

According to Pru, the year is 1811, and that is a *fact*. She seems quite certain of that. Well, here's another fact: Pru and her mother think I'm a certifiable nut. But if Pru is right, and this is 1811, and I'm right, and I've traveled back in time, *and* if Ms. Drummond is right about the historical happenings, all *heck* is going to break loose again soon.

This morning, Mrs. Keeler was quite grumpy, and I felt tired, too. I had barely closed my eyes and then it was morning.

"Wake up, Zoey," Pru said. "It is time to rise."

"No, not yet," I murmured, trying to pull the quilts over my head. "It's still dark. I don't want to get up."

"Zoey," Mrs. Keeler said with a sharp edge to her voice.

"What?" I said from under my covers. "I mean, ma'am?"

"Arise. You must help Prudence with the wood and

water. When the sun is up, everyone rises. There is work to be done."

"Wood? What do you mean wood?" I poked my head out.

Pru was trying not to laugh, which was a good thing, as her mother obviously was not in the mood for joking around about something as serious as wood.

"We must chop wood for our fire and bring water from the creek," Pru told me.

I pushed my head farther out from under the quilt and peered at her. "What about all that wood stacked over there?" I pointed toward the pile stacked by what used to be their cabin.

"We save that for truly inclement weather," Mrs. Keeler said.

"Well, what kind of weather is this?" I asked.

"Zoey!" Pru said.

I looked at her. I guess I did sound sassy.

"Mama means we save that wood for when it snows. And, yes, we have to tote the water from the creek as well," Pru said. "Surely you did these things for your own family?"

I pointed again at that beautiful, tall woodpile and shook my head, dumbfounded and, for once, speechless.

Pru gave me an ax and pointed toward the woods. "Chop as much wood as you can," she said, as if I did this every day. "Find fallen logs and chop them into kindling."

I took the ax and went a few feet into the woods. I

approached a small tree that had fallen. I tried hitting it with the ax. Nothing happened except that I missed cutting my foot off at the ankle by about a millimeter.

After a while, Pru came out and showed me how to hold the ax over my head and swing down, hard. Then you keep hitting the log in the same spot until you cut it in half. I think I chopped four pieces of kindling today. Not four logs. Four pieces of kindling. I'm so sore I can hardly move.

And there were other chores, too, like toting water, stoking the fire, and loading the wagon. There was one bright spot in the day: Mrs. Keeler seems ready to get out of here as soon as possible. We might not have to wait for the absent Mr. Keeler.

After my less than stellar attempts at chores. I beckoned to Pru. "Let's see what we can find to eat in your house," I said.

"We must be careful not to get hurt," Pru said.

We made our way into the rubble. There were several sacks of goods that had fallen to the floor. Some of them had burst open.

I took a couple of aprons that I found hanging on a peg by the chimney and placed two open bags of grain in each one and tied them up. I found a sackful of sugar that was still usable, and a tin of coffee, which cheered me up.

There was no way to get into the cellar. Logs and debris were blocking the hole in the floor. My stomach growled and rumbled. "Man, that's loud!" I said, picking up the makeshift bags. The rumbling grew louder. *Oh, please, no, not again!*

Pru and I grabbed the aprons and picked our way through the rubble as fast as we could. The ground began shaking and bucking as we ran across the dirt yard and threw ourselves into balls on the ground. I could hear the mule braying and Mrs. Keeler screaming, too.

I want to go home. I want to go home. I want to go home, I prayed as the world around me went into convulsions.

Prudence

17 December 1811 (continued)

This morning was long and hard. We repaired the wagon as best we could and loaded many things into it. I cannot dare to believe that Mama will just take us away, but she seems most determined. We picked through the remains of our home and salvaged what we could before another earthquake had us huddling together on the ground, waiting it out. We packed many blankets and extra clothes into the wagon, along with some household goods and some of our surplus food items, such as sugar, flour, fruits, vegetables, and lard. We will continue packing tomorrow.

My new friend did attempt to help us, though her efforts were not successful. She does not know how to handle an ax. After an hour, she had managed to chop one log in half and split that half into four small pieces of kindling. I set her to the task of toting water from the creek. The bucket left the creek lapping full and by the time it reached us, most of the water from the bucket was on Zoey. I helped her with that, too.

I tried not to let Mama see how useless Zoey is to us with chores. I believe Zoey will learn, given time.

During chores, Zoey mumbled to herself quite a bit about earthquakes and the Mississippi and needing to leave the area, and whether it can truly be 1811—which, of course, I know it is, having been born in 1799 and having lived through every year of this new century.

Despite our best efforts, Mama was shivering uncontrollably throughout the morning. I could tell that she was in pain, but I wanted to scream at her to get up and be strong. And what of the baby? Is the baby in danger now?

After Zoey and I left the cabin, the earthquakes continued for some time, with only a few moments of quiet in between. We sat up after the first assault and tried to get our bearings, but when the earth began quaking again, more violently than before, Mama screamed. I threw my body over hers as chunks of earth and sand and coal began exploding out of the ground around us. More trees cracked and groaned, and the screams of wild animals mingled with Mama's and my own, and those of Zoey as well. King George brayed and bucked in a wild circle.

All around us, the earth rolled in waves, like wind over a field of grass. I almost felt hypnotized by the dreadful beauty of it, but the insistent screeching of animals and the cracking of tree limbs brought home to me the horror of our situation. I held my moaning mother for what seemed like hours until the earth beneath us slowed and stopped moving.

"Mrs. Keeler," Zoey said, crawling over to Mama and me, "we have to get out of here. I think we need to forget about packing up and just go. Can't we just head for the fort now?"

"I want to leave, but what if your papa comes home?" Mama said, her voice a plaintive wail. She gripped my arm so hard it hurt. "If we are not here, he might think . . . that we have died!" Mama began to cry in earnest. I patted her hands.

"If we don't leave, for sure we'll be dead!" Zoey said. "This land we're on is going to be a lake soon!"

Mama wiped her eyes on my dress. She did look peaked, I could see, truly quite ill. "I know that it is too dangerous to wait for him here, although I had hoped these earthquakes would cease. I don't know if I can make it to the fort, though." Mama was quiet for a moment. "What about the steamboat, Prudence?" she said. Her voice was weak. "Mayhap we should travel to Little Prairie and see if we can intercept the steamboat." Mama collapsed as if she had no energy for even one more word.

"Are you talking about the *New Orleans*?" Zoey said. She seemed quite agitated.

"Mama," I said, "do you think we should try to make it to the *New Orleans*?"

"Yes, dear. I do not know if I can walk, though."

Zoey shook her head. "There's no point."

"Why? Why do you say that, Zoey? You cannot know everything!" I knew I was shouting in a most unladylike fashion, but I was weary of Zoey's never-ending font of knowledge. "I wish you would go back where you came from!"

Zoey's face crumpled. I felt horrid. I never had hurt anyone's feelings on purpose before.

Zoey began to cry silently. Tears rolled down her face. "I wish I could go back where I came from, too, Pru," she said. "But I don't know how!"

"Perhaps if they see the condition I am in, girls, the good Roosevelts will allow us to board the *New Orleans* and journey to Natchez." Mama had a pitiful look of hope on her face that made me want to weep.

"I don't think it will work," Zoey said. She slapped her forehead. "I wish I had finished reading my homework like I was supposed to," she said. "I think there's going to be a whole horde of people wanting to get on that boat."

"But is it not worth a try?" I asked.

Zoey

December 18

Way back in the day, or should I say *forward* in the day, Ms. Drummond told us that the official state animal of Tennessee is the raccoon. And I would happily chow down on one right now if it crossed my path. I'm starving!

Before we left, Pru and I discussed the best way to travel. Mrs. Keeler wanted to drag the wagon along, but Pru and I thought we should travel light.

Whinny-ah-haw! the mule brayed as I approached the wagon to look at what we'd already packed. He stood behind the falling-down fence. I stopped and looked at him. He was big and scary. What had I learned about mules when Jillian and I went to Mule Day? Pack mules could carry or pull a lot of stuff. Mules were agile and could jump over fallen trees. Mules were stubborn.

Whinny-ah-haw! the mule brayed again.

"You're not a stubborn old coot, are you?" I

reached across the fence with my hand upturned and to my delight, he nuzzled my palm. "You're a good-looking thing," I told him. I stroked his white face and coarse brown mane. "For a mule, that is. You didn't run off and leave us like those other silly animals, did you?" We hadn't seen hide nor hair of the cow, the pigs, or the chickens since the earthquakes destroyed the barn.

"We can use the mule to carry our stuff," I called to Pru. "What's his name, anyway?"

"King George," Pru said. "Papa said he is as stubborn as King George of England."

"Oh, hey! You mean old King George the third, who taxed us to death?"

"Yes, but now he is a sick old man. The broadsides say he is going mad," Pru said.

"He's not insane," I said, "he's sick with—"

"You talk nonsense, girl," Mrs. Keeler interrupted us.

I decided not to explain any further. She wouldn't believe me anyway. "About King George," I said, pointing to the mule.

"Enough about that tyrant!" Mrs. Keeler said. "We have more important things to worry about!"

"I meant the mule!" I said.

We all looked at each other for a long time. Then we all began to laugh. It felt really good to see Mrs. Keeler laugh for a change, and Pru, too.

"Maybe you could ride on him, Mrs. Keeler," I said. "If it wouldn't be too uncomfortable for you."

"That is the most sensible thing you have said, Miss

Zoey," Mrs. Keeler said. Her voice sounded softer. Maybe someday she'll like me.

We got King George ready, left a note for Pru's father, and we were on the move all day. It has been very slow going. Everywhere we look, trees are down; there are holes in the ground, with boiling sand and rocks erupting from them—and with all the vapors, it's hard to see two feet in front of our faces.

I wish you were here, Dad. And you, too, Mom. My horizons have been broadened about as much as I can stand, that's for sure. I've never felt so homesick in my life—even more homesick than I did during the two weeks I spent at Camp Ocoee when I was ten and had poison ivy the whole time. I've got to figure out a way to get out of here, but it just boggles my mind!

Pru built a nifty trap out of sticks and a woven basket when we stopped to rest. She said her old friend Kalopin helped her learn to trap. Mrs. Keeler made a face at this little tidbit, so I guess Kalopin is a Native American. She seems to have a real thing about the Indians, which makes me feel strange. I wonder how she would like Grandma Cope. But who could not like Grandma? Even if she is Native American?

"Today we will make it to Little Prairie," Prudence said as she opened the trap.

"Did we catch anything?" I asked. My stomach felt like it was touching my backbone, I was so hungry.

"Yes, a wild duck," Prudence said with a good deal of satisfaction.

"Great," I said, and looked into the trap. "Wait a minute! It's still alive!"

"Of course, Zoey. We only trapped it. Now we have to wring its neck and pluck it so that we can cook it over the fire." Prudence acted very matter-of-fact about it all.

I felt the bile rise in my throat. I jumped away from the trap and ran a few feet. Bending over, I threw up what little was in my stomach and then got the dry heaves for good measure. Prudence patted my back, and then she handed me a little scrap of cloth to wipe my mouth. This was so much like something Jillian would have done that I felt sick all over again. Sick with missing home.

"Do not worry, Zoey," Pru said to me. "I will pluck and cook this bird."

"You're going to have to," I told her. "The only birds I ever eat are chicken parts that have already been pressed into nuggets. Not birds I've just seen pecking at the ground."

I watched, a bit in awe of her skill, as Pru snapped the bird's neck, removed its internal organs, and boiled the body. After that, the feathers came off easily.

"This was good, Pru," I told her a couple of hours later. And it was delicious, as hungry as I had been. "A little tough and kind of greasy, but good." I took a long drink of burnt coffee. Some flavored creamer would have been a nice touch, but beggars not being choosers and all that, I kept my mouth shut.

"Can you get King George ready for the night, Zoey?" Pru said. "He worked very hard today."

"Sure, what do I do?" I tried to sound confident, but my insides quaked a bit at the thought of getting too close to the huge beast.

"Put a blanket over him, and tie him to that tree. Then give him some grain," Pru told me.

I approached the mule. "Hey, Georgie-porgie," I said. King George brayed and stomped his back hoof. "Hungry? Okay, boy."

"That mule likes you," Pru said with a laugh. "Papa will be surprised. He said King George does not like anyone."

"Well, George here doesn't have a whole lot of friends to choose from," I said. I didn't, either, really, but Pru was okay for someone from the past. The ground rumbled and several small tremors shook the area.

"Zoey, maybe you should not tie King George up. If a bad quake should happen, he might injure himself," Pru called to me.

"Good thinking, Pru," I said. I stroked the mule's soft nose. "It's like he knows he's helping us."

"Nonsense," said Mrs. Keeler, but the corners of her mouth seemed to turn up a little. "Animals do not understand humans."

"Animals can and do have feelings, Papa says," Pru said in a voice as close to being smart-mouthed as I had heard her use. "What about your old dog, Jim, that you had as a child?"

"Jim was a dog. King George is a mule." But Mrs. Keeler didn't sound harsh. "And Jim was special."

"I used to have a dog," I said. "His name was Rascal.

But I didn't spend enough time playing with him. Mom gave him to a sick kid down the street." I was quiet for a minute. "I do have a hamster now. His name's Hamhock."

Mrs. Keeler snorted at that and then covered her mouth.

"Hamhock's not much company, though. He sleeps a lot. I hope Mom's taking care of him." I looked at the mule. "Maybe that's why I like old King George. I can appreciate his finer qualities now that I'm not distracted by the phone and the TV."

If I were home right now, I'd play with Hamhock. And I'd spend a lot more time talking to Mom and Dad. And Grandma Cope. My eyes are tearing up. Why didn't I let them come on my field trip?

Prudence

19 December 1811

This morning we reached Little Prairie. I cannot describe my shock. We settled Mama on the ground, against the stump of a tree. There was no one about. Cabins were sunk into the ground. Trees were sheared off. Black buzzards and vultures roosted in the shattered remains of the trees, waiting to feed on the dead. I shivered as I looked into their shiny black eyes.

"I told you, Pru," Zoey said as we walked away from Mama. "We need to get out of here."

"We have no way to know if the *New Orleans* has passed by," I insisted.

"But what if they won't help us?" Zoey asked in a defiant tone.

"We have to try, if only for Mama!" I shouted. "I must take care of her!"

Zoey looked stricken, and she blushed. "I suppose you're right, Pru. I'm sorry. We do have to try. I *think* I know what happened here, but I could be wrong.

Grandma Cope said that things happen for a reason, but sometimes, with enough will and hard work, we can change things. Maybe that's why I'm here. I don't know." Zoey looked sad.

"Look, Zoey!" I said, hoping to cheer her up. A small group of men, women, and children were coming out of the woods and making their way to the river. "Let us go and speak with them. They may know what is happening elsewhere." Zoey and I hurried toward them.

"Good day. Has the *New Orleans* passed yet?" a weary-looking woman asked us.

"Good day to you, ma'am. I do not believe so," I answered. "I cannot be sure."

"We hope to board the steamboat and travel to Natchez," the woman said.

"We hope to as well," I answered. I pointed to Mama, who rested against the tree stump with her eyes closed. It worried me that she seemed so unaware of what was happening around her.

The woman's eyes flickered toward Mama and back to Zoey and me. "Does she have the influenza? Or the pox?" she asked as she pulled her cloak more closely about her and stepped back.

"No, no, she is just . . . feeling poorly," I insisted.

"She's going to have a baby soon," Zoey said. I looked at her in shock. My mother's condition is something people simply do not talk about in public.

"Zoey!" I said as the woman stepped farther away.

"But she's not sick! I don't want people acting like

we're contagious," Zoey said. "Having a baby is the most natural thing in the world," she continued. "My mom always says so."

"Please, Zoey!" I said. "We do not discuss such things in polite society."

I was most relieved when Zoey closed her mouth, but I could see by the glint in my new friend's eyes that something else, probably equally inappropriate, was about to pour forth.

"Let us go and see how Mama is faring," I said, taking Zoey by the arm.

We found Mama sitting up a bit more, looking a little stronger. "Are you having pains, Mrs. Keeler?" Zoey asked.

"Zoey!" I shouted.

Zoey looked back and forth between Mama and me. "Did I say something wrong?"

"I told you we must not talk about Mama's delicate condition."

Zoey stood up and walked away from us. She appeared to be quite agitated. When she came back, she hunkered down in front of Mama and me. "Look," she said. "Maybe I wasn't raised to be as polite in society as the two of you. But where I come from, having babies is no big deal."

I started to interrupt her, but stopped when she held up her hand. "No, Pru, you have to listen to me. Your mom could have the baby sooner than expected, and we need to be prepared. We all can't sit around and act like it's not going to happen."

"My pains have lessened somewhat, Zoey," Mama said. "I am feeling stronger."

"Maybe you're having false labor, Mrs. Keeler? Those practice pains? My mom told me about them. When are you due?"

Mama blushed. I held her hand. I knew how hard it was for Mama to discuss such a private matter, and with someone she did not know or trust.

"I believe the babe should come in February," Mama said. Her face flamed again. "But I worry because I have been having . . . many pains. I feel so very weak."

"I'm sorry to embarrass you, Mrs. Keeler, but we should be thinking about all this, you know? Where I come from, most ladies get to the hospital as soon as they're having their pains and let the doctors take over." Zoey shivered and picked up a quilt, throwing it over her head and wrapping it around her shoulders. "Don't you need to get to the doctor?"

"What do you know of hospitals or doctors?" Mama said. "Do the red men have hospitals and doctors?" She stood up and moved to the fire, walking with careful, deliberate steps. I rushed to help her when she stopped and clutched her belly.

"Look, Mrs. Keeler, I don't know much about the Native Americans and how they practice medicine, but we do need some help," Zoey said.

"Zoey," I warned, motioning to my mother. "There are no doctors in this area. Only Indian midwives, but Mama doesn't want—"

"I don't want any squaw helping me," Mama said through gritted teeth. She slumped down onto a log by the fire. "I want . . . I want my husband." Mama put her face in her hands and began to cry. I dropped to the ground at her feet and wrapped my arms around her.

Zoey moved closer to me and Mama. "Isn't there *any* place we can go for help?"

"Zoey," I said. This time my voice was sharp. I knew my new friend could hear the warning in my tone because her mouth clapped shut. "This is Obion, in the middle of Chickasaw Country. There are no doctors here. That is why we must pray for passage on the steamboat."

"The steamboat will take us to Natchez," Mama said. "I am certain that if they see my . . . my condition, they will take me on board."

"I don't think so, Mrs. Keeler, but I do understand why you're holding out hope." Zoey looked quite earnest.

"We need to think about shelter for the night," I said. "What if we lean some of these fallen logs against the tree and stretch a hide over it?"

"Now, that's good thinking, Pru," Zoey said, and smiled her brilliant smile at me. I had not noticed before, but Zoey has the whitest, most perfectly straight teeth I have ever seen. After Kalopin's. She looked around. "It's getting darker. We should spread a hide or blanket on the ground, too, to help keep us dry."

"That is a good idea," I said.

Zoey smiled. "I was a Girl Scout, once upon a time,

and we used to go camping," she said as she began looking around for pieces of wood. "I never thought I'd put
all that wilderness training to this much use, though."

"Were you a scout for the Indians?" Mama asked.

Zoey just sighed and shook her head at us.

Zoey

We are in Little Prairie. Others are here, too, refugees from all over the area, it seems. All of us are waiting for the steamboat, the *New Orleans*. These people believe that it will be their salvation, but I've got news for them.

I sat down by Mrs. Keeler and looked her in the eyes. I was tired of her believing I was an Indian captive. Never in my life had it been so important for someone to believe I was telling the truth. That was when I heard a chugging sound out on the river. Pru heard it, too.

We jumped up and ran for the riverbank to look for the *New Orleans*. People shouted to each other above the noise of the approaching steamboat, all making plans for what they would do when they reached Natchez.

When the steamboat was in the middle of the channel, it slowed. Smoke billowed from it. Several men lowered a flatboat over the side and began paddling toward the shoreline. The people on land shouted their excitement. Many men and some women waded out into the water to help pull the flatboat onto shore when it got close.

"Will Mr. Roosevelt take on any passengers?" Pru shouted. I seethed inside as the woman who'd been afraid she might catch a germ from us maneuvered herself in front of Pru. I pushed my way to Pru and pulled her by the arm through the crowd to stand in front of the steamboat crew.

A large man with a red face looked at us. "No, miss, we apologize. Mr. Roosevelt cannot take any passengers aboard. We fear the *New Orleans* will capsize."

"Not even one small woman who is about to have a baby?" I pleaded. "She needs help!"

"Mrs. Roosevelt has had her own baby since they began this trip. I don't think she is up to having extra passengers on board, even if we weren't afraid the boat might sink," the big, red-faced man told us.

"Mayhap Mrs. Roosevelt will be sympathetic to Mama because of her delicate condition," Prudence said, and then blushed.

"Yes, she's pregnant, and she needs to see a doctor!" I added. What was wrong with these people?

A second man, skinny as a whippet and with an ugly scar on his face, smirked at us. I turned to see Pru hiding her face in her hands. I knew it was because I had said the unmentionable word again.

" 'Bout to pop, eh?" the skinny man said, and then spat. I jumped back from the black liquid that the man had let fly.

"Yuck," I muttered, looking at the disgusting blob on the ground at my feet. "Chewing that stuff is bad for your health," I told the skinny man. I couldn't help myself.

The man wiped his mouth on a greasy sleeve. His lips parted in a nasty little grin.

"And your teeth," I added, looking at the blackened stubs and shivering.

"Why, you little . . . ," the man said, advancing toward me.

"Watch it, Turlock," the bigger man said. "Leave the young ladies alone."

"Listen, sir," I said, turning toward the bigger man. "This girl's mother is in a bad way. You've got to help her!"

"Miss, if we take one woman aboard, we will have to take all the women aboard. We simply cannot help you."

"But what are we supposed to do?" Pru said. "Everything we own has been destroyed!"

The big man with the red face touched Prudence on the arm. "We know it is bad. But I am not the captain of the boat. I have to follow my orders. We have come ashore to get firewood. We plan to see what damage the boat has sustained. Within a few days, we will be on our way." He smiled kindly at Pru. "I'm sorry, miss. Truly I am."

The men pushed through the crowd and began gathering fallen branches. They did not respond to the many women who crowded around them, begging for passage. I felt sick.

Several of the men who had waited for the arrival of the *New Orleans* waded out into the water and began swimming toward the steamboat. As they neared the boat, a member of the crew stepped to the railing and pointed a long rifle at them. After much shouting back and forth, the men swam back to shore and clambered out of the water. Many of them gathered their families around them and began to walk away from the destroyed town of Little Prairie, disappearing into the woods from which they had come.

I'd been afraid this would happen, and now we had to come up with a new plan. What would Grandma Cope do? I did know one thing. It was time to talk to Mrs. Keeler. She had to know the truth. I walked back toward her, followed by Pru.

"I was never an Indian scout," I said. I looked at Mrs. Keeler and took a deep breath. "Indians never kidnapped me during any raid. I came here from the future. I live in Nashville, Tennessee. Somehow I've been thrown back in time. There was a storm and lightning, and I was struck and . . . well, I don't really know *how* it happened, but it happened."

Mrs. Keeler looked at me. "I will not believe such talk. It sounds like blasphemy. Like witchery!"

"I know it is hard for you to believe, but it is true." I got up and went to King George. I had hidden my backpack with all the extra clothes and blankets. I took it out and brought it back to Mrs. Keeler and Pru. I unzipped my pack while Pru looked at it in amazement. It struck me that zippers were probably not around in 1811. Reaching inside, I pulled out Mike's old book and my social studies book. I held my textbook up so they could see the cover. On the front were pictures of people of all different cultures. Superimposed on it were a jet in flight, a passenger train speeding through a city, and the New York skyline.

"What . . . what is that?" Pru asked, pointing at the airplane.

"It's an airplane. It flies through the sky. It can take people from the United States to Europe." I watched as Pru's eyes grew huge.

"People can fly through the sky?" she said.

I took a deep breath. "Prudence, people can go to the *moon*. They fly there in a rocket."

Mrs. Keeler looked like she was about to pass out. Prudence looked pale but excited. "What is that?" she asked, pointing at the skyline picture.

"That is New York City," I explained. "The buildings there look like they touch the sky. They're called skyscrapers."

"What do people do in those buildings?" Pru asked.

"Work!"

"I do not understand," Pru whispered.

"Millions of people live and work in New York City. Heck, in Nashville, there are more than half a million people."

"Oh, my goodness!" Pru exclaimed. "Papa says that our Congress requires a territory to have at least sixty thousand people to apply for statehood. He says that when Tennessee applied, it barely had enough people to meet the requirement."

Now it was my turn to feel stunned. "Wow, Pru, that's so cool," I said, and shook my head.

We were all silent for a few minutes. "Now do you believe me? Indians never kidnapped me. I learned about what happened here in social studies class in school. I swear. On my honor."

Prudence

22 December 1811

Mama is beset with worry. It has been a few hours since the steamboat chugged away from what remained of Little Prairie. For three days the men gathered wood, but they allowed no one on the boat. I sit by Mama, writing of what has happened and feeding twigs into the small fire. My heart feels heavy in my chest. I had hoped with all my might that the *New Orleans* would take us aboard, or at the least, give Mama passage to Natchez and a doctor. It was a bitter blow that Mr. Roosevelt will let no one travel with him to safety.

Zoey sits across from us. She has changed out of the dress I loaned her and back into her leathers. She pulled her long, dark hair into two braids and looks more like an Indian than ever, I think. I know that Mama thinks so as well. Mama has not allowed herself to look at Zoey since she changed out of the dress. I know Mama cannot abide a woman wearing britches. It is almost a sin, in her eyes.

She still does not accept Zoey's story, and the way Zoey looks now, it is easy to understand why. And yet, as much as I do not want to believe that Zoey is a girl who was born nearly two hundred years in the future, I cannot help thinking she is telling me the truth. How else to explain the book she has, supposedly written in 1925, and how she knew that we would not receive help from the *New Orleans*?

Later in the day

Zoey tapped me on the shoulder, interrupting my writing.

"We need to hurry and get to the fort," she said for what seemed to me like the hundredth time. "There's bound to be help available there. That's what forts are for—to protect people."

"I do not want to cross the Mississippi River on a small boat," Mama said. "Prudence and I cannot swim, and a small boat will be very dangerous. If the river continues to rage as it does here at Little Prairie each time there is an earthquake, it will be deadly. What will happen to us all if we are in the middle of the river and an earthquake strikes?"

"What will happen to us if we stay here?" I asked.

"We might drown either way," Zoey said. "But we need to cross the river before February. Things are going to get seriously bad in February. Mike's book says—"

"We could attempt to cross on a raft," I said to

Mama, interrupting Zoey. "If we go to a place where we can see islands in the water, we can let King George pull the raft from the shore to an island and then on to the other shore."

"You do not know what you are talking about, Prudence," Mama said. "What if the water is too deep for that mule?"

"He'll swim, I know he will," Zoey said.

"What do you know of mules?" Mama said. I know that she did not intend to be mean to Zoey, but she sounded a bit snappish, even to me.

"Do not mind Mama," I said to Zoey. "She feels poorly."

Zoey's face reddened and her eyes filled with tears. She stood up and walked away from Mama and me, over to where King George stood.

"Mama, you were unkind to Zoey. She means well," I whispered to her.

"That girl talks nonsense. She is addled. I cannot trust a thing she says," Mama said. "I still do not know what to make of the strange stories she tells us. What would Papa think?"

"We cannot spend our lives waiting for Papa to tell us what to do!" I said, and stood up. "We have to decide things on our own."

"Prudence Charity Keeler! I will not have you speak to me in such a disrespectful fashion."

"I am deeply sorry, Mama. I do not mean any disrespect. I do speak the truth, though. Papa is not here to help us. I think we need to consider what Zoey says.

Please think about it, Mama." I walked toward Zoey and King George, leaving Mama sitting alone.

Later, Zoey and I huddled on either side of Mama, trying to warm her. In front of us, a small fire burned. It allowed us to see only a few feet around ourselves. The air was foggy with vapors, and it smelled worse than the time as a little girl that I found the rotten eggs that had rolled under the chicken coop. I cracked them open with a rock to see if chicks would appear. None did, but the smell lasted for several days.

I long for those simple days now. I cannot believe I was ever bored or prayed for excitement. Since the earthquakes began, my life has been one of constant excitement, but of a fearful sort. Some moments, I find myself burning with anger at Papa for leaving us. Then I wish that he would find us and take all of my worries— and Mama's— off my shoulders.

And Kalopin. I wonder where he is, and if Laughing Eyes is with him. Are these terrifying earthquakes the result of Copiah's curse? Is Kalopin dead? I pray not.

24 December 1811

We left Little Prairie yesterday, after Mama regained some of her strength. Now it is Christmas Eve and we are attempting to make it to the fort, to see if Papa is there. I hope there will be passage across the river. The crossing at Little Prairie appeared treacherous.

Zoey argued against going back to the area around our old home, for it soon will be underwater. I am grateful that Mama appeared to agree with her that the fort is our best choice.

We will walk as far as we can today, but it will not be far enough, Zoey says. Mama can move only so fast, though, due to her condition. The baby shows no immediate sign of coming, thank the good Lord, though Mama continues to experience pains. If Mama and the baby can hold on until we reach the fort, it will be a blessing.

It is hard to believe that it is Christmas Eve and we are not in our new home with Papa! Where is he? I wonder, at least every other minute. I hope he is safe and warm tonight. Perhaps he camps with some Indians.

We have stopped to rest and Mama is fixing supper. It is nice to see her moving about like her old self. Zoey and I will go and check the traps I made, to see if we caught anything. I will write more later.

Later in the day

"Supper is ready, girls," Mama called to us.

Zoey and I looked up from the traps we were repairing. Earlier, we checked the traps that we had set up the day before. When we found nothing, it was disheartening.

But Mama had not been discouraged. She was feeling somewhat more energetic and went out with the long rifle. When she returned, her bag looked heavy.

She assured us that she had shot something for our Christmas meal.

Zoey paled at this news. Although she knows that we must often shoot animals in order to eat, I know she does not like hunting.

"Prudence, will you pray?" Mama said as we all sat down on the hide she had spread on the ground. In an effort to be festive, Mama had placed pinecones and branches with red berries around the bark tray that held our meal in the middle of the hide. We had found other flat pieces of bark to make plates.

"Dear Lord, bless this food and make it nourishing unto our bodies. Bless the poor souls who have nothing to eat on this day. Keep Papa safe. Let us all be reunited soon. Amen." I sniffled and wiped my eyes.

"It's going to be all right, Pru," Zoey said.

"I miss my papa," I answered. "Where could he be?"

"I do not know where Papa is, but I am most certain that he is doing all in his power to return to us, Prudence," Mama said. "We must continue to have faith. I know he would want us to be strong." Mama passed a hand over her eyes. "Now let us eat before the food becomes cold."

She lifted the piece of cloth that covered the makeshift platter. A steaming, fire-cooked piece of meat was in the center of the platter, surrounded by steamed yams and carrots from the bag we had brought with us.

"Mama, that looks delicious!" I exclaimed.

"It looks like a big rat," Zoey said. "What is it? Or do I want to know?"

I scowled at Zoey, knowing Mama would think she was quite rude. "It is possum," I said. "It is a bit greasy, but good, especially with the vegetables."

Zoey turned white and then green right before my eyes. She began making small gagging sounds before she leaped to her feet and dashed to the edge of the clearing. For a few moments, she heaved, leaning against a tree.

Mama shook her head in disgust. "Zoey, you have a mighty weak stomach."

"I'm sorry," Zoey called from the tree. "I cannot eat a possum."

"Come and have some vegetables, Zoey," I said. "I know you must be hungry."

Zoey came back to where Mama had spread our meal out. "Don't you eat turkey for holidays?" she asked me and Mama. "With deviled eggs and cranberry sauce?"

"Have you seen any turkeys wandering around?" Mama said. "We eat what there is to eat. The good Lord provides."

"What about a Christmas tree?" Zoey asked. "Do you ever decorate one? When you're not having earth-quakes, I mean?"

"I have heard of Christmas trees," Mama said, "but I have never seen one."

"What do they look like?" I asked.

Zoey took a bite of yams and chewed. "Our tree was— I mean is—beautiful. Mom hangs the kinds of lights that blink on and off. We have ornaments from when my parents were kids, things they made, and things I've made, too. And tinsel. And a big star on the top." She sighed.

"What do you do with the tree?" Mama said. I could see that she did not want to appear too interested, but I was glad she had asked about the tree.

"We set it up in the house, usually around December fifteenth or so. On Christmas Eve, when I go to bed, Mom and Dad rustle around under there and put out all the presents Santa Claus has brought me. I don't believe in Santa anymore, but Mom says, 'If you want him to come, you have to have faith.' "

"Who is Santa Claus?" I said.

"He's a jolly old elf in a red suit," Zoey said.

I did not know what to make of this, but then I often do not know what to make of Zoey's fantastical tales.

She picked at her vegetables for a bit. "What do you do for Christmas?"

"We praise God," Mama said. "We go to church."

"Do you exchange presents?" Zoey asked.

"We do not celebrate Christmas that way. Now eat," Mama said.

"That is not true, Mama," I shot back. "We do exchange presents, and you know it!" It was rude of me to shout at Mama, I know, but she angered me with her dismissal of Zoey's Christmas celebrations.

"I am only saying, Prudence, that our way of remembering Christmas seems a more sober event than foolishness with trees and elves and the like."

"Mama, you have lost your sense of fun, and you are being rude!" I said. "Remember how we always sing hymns and carols with Papa on Christmas Eve, and pop corn over the fire?" I turned to Zoey. "Before we go to bed, Papa always reads the nativity story to us from the Bible. We *do* celebrate Christmas!" I felt as if I might cry thinking of the holidays in front of the fire with Papa—and Mama—in better times.

"It's okay," Zoey interjected. "I can see where your mom is coming from. What I'm talking about probably seems like a bunch of silliness. But it's always such a fun day hanging out with my family, and exchanging presents with my best friend, Jillian, in the afternoon." She sighed again. "Now, in the situation we're in, I'd be happy just to be home celebrating Christmas, even without presents."

Zoey got up again and walked away from the meal.

"Mama, it is unkind of you to say those things," I said.

"Prudence! You dare to tell me how I should speak?" Mama's face turned bright red.

"I am most sorry, Mama. But it seems to me that you want to hurt Zoey. She cannot help that she is different from us. She cannot help that we do not understand most of what she speaks about. I am certain that she does not understand most of the things we speak about, either. But she is lost."

"*We* are lost, Prudence! We are lost!" Mama put her head in her hands and began to cry.

"Mama, don't cry, please! We are lost, true. But we have each other. Zoey has no one."

Zoey

December 25, 1811

It's Christmas Day. I wonder what Mom and Dad are doing. Are they looking for me? Did they watch *It's a Wonderful Life* and *A Christmas Story* without me? Did they go caroling with all our neighbors and their kids and then have hot chocolate by the fire? Or are they still fighting? Did they spend Christmas alone? I wish I knew how Grandma Cope was doing right now, too. I worry about how frantic they all must be that I'm gone.

I'd give my eyeteeth for some spiral-sliced ham and a big old turkey leg right now. I could not bring myself to eat that possum last night. It might be a delicacy to some folks, but it looked like something out of a scary movie to me.

It's early, and I'm writing as I wait for Pru and her mother to wake up. I'm sitting by the fire I stoked earlier, wrapped in an old quilt. The sun is coming up, something I hardly *ever* saw in my old life! I thought a lot about what Mrs. Keeler said yesterday. I want to show her that I'm not as strange as she thinks I am. And I know it will make Pru happy when she sees what I have done for her! Oh! They're waking up. More later.

Later

Mrs. Keeler stirred first, moaning a bit and then opening her eyes. I'll bet sleeping on the hard ground when your belly is as big as Mrs. Keeler's does not make for a good night's rest. Finally, she sat up. I jumped up and went over to help her to her feet. "Here's coffee for you," I said, handing her a cup.

"Thank you, Zoey. How nice of you to make the coffee for me this morning," she said between sips. She grimaced a bit, then smiled. "It is certainly hot. And strong."

"Merry Christmas, Mrs. Keeler," I said.

"And a blessed Christmas to you," Mrs. Keeler told me. She even smiled at me. Well, a little.

"Wake up, Pru!" I said, shaking her shoulder. "Merry Christmas!" I handed Pru a cup of coffee, too, and gave her about thirty seconds to open her eyes.

"Come and look," I said when they both appeared to be awake. I led them away from the fire and into the woods a bit and pointed.

There in the woods was a tiny evergreen. On its sparse branches, I had tied bits of material into bows. Beneath the tree were two items wrapped in pages that I had torn out of my social studies book.

"See, Santa Claus came last night!" I said. I took Pru and Mrs. Keeler by the hands and led them to the tree. "He brought you presents."

"Such nonsense," Mrs. Keeler said, but she didn't walk away. And that half smile was still trying to break loose on her face.

"Oh, Zoey, this Christmas tree is beautiful," Pru said, and clapped. Her eyes shone.

"Here's a present for you, Mrs. Keeler, and one for you, Pru," I said. I placed the gifts in their hands. "Open them!"

Pru unfolded the pages I had wrapped around her gift. Inside were two of my ink pens, a couple of sparkly hair barrettes with rhinestones embedded in them, and a toboggan hat with the official Tennessee Titans logo embroidered on it.

"I know those pens won't last forever, but I would love for you to use them while they do," I said to Pru. "If I ever get back home, I can buy dozens of them."

"These gifts are beautiful," Pru said. "Thank you, Zoey." She turned to her mother. "Mama, open your gift!"

Mrs. Keeler unwrapped her presents and considered them for a moment. I had given her my fur-lined gloves and a tube of lip balm. Different emotions warred on her face. She looked at me. "Thank you for these gifts. These gloves look warm."

"Not to worry, Mrs. Keeler," I said. "That's faux fur in those gloves. I mean, it isn't real. I didn't kill anything to make them," I hurried to assure her.

At that, Mrs. Keeler laughed. "I am most certain of that, Zoey. Hmm," she continued. "What do I do with this?" she asked, holding up the lip balm.

"You put it on your lips to keep them soft. It smells like strawberries."

"Better than my salve?" Mrs. Keeler asked with a smile.

She was actually making a joke! I didn't know if I felt like laughing or crying. "Put your gloves on," I urged her.

Mrs. Keeler slipped the gloves onto her hands. "Oh my, yes, these are warm," she said, her pleasure evident.

"Put on your hat, Pru!" I turned to my friend. "Let's see how you look!"

Prudence pulled the knit hat down on her head. I reached over and adjusted it so that the Titans logo was in the front.

"You look wonderful," I said. "Very sporty and modern. And pretty!"

Pru smiled at me, and for a moment, I could see how she would look in my time, wearing jeans and a cool coat with her hat, sledding with my friends down the big hill behind Grandma Cope's house.

"How about some mush with sugar?" Mrs. Keeler said as we made our way back to the fire.

"That sounds edible," I said. "What else is in it?"

"Just some rice." Pru laughed.

"Oh, that's just like the breakfasts Grandma Cope used to make me! She would add butter, milk, and sugar to rice that was left over from our dinner the night before."

"Your grandmother sounds nice," Pru said.

"She was nice. She *is* nice. I miss her a lot." My heart hurt at that.

"I hope that you will see her again, Zoey," Pru said.

"Yeah, me too. I really do."

January 5, 1812

We were all sick with something after Christmas and had to make camp for several days and wait it out. I hesitated to ask if it was from something we ate, but we were all laid low with stomach pains, and then sneezing, coughing, and fever. Mrs. Keeler was so ill that Pru and I were frantic, but she turned the corner a few days ago.

Now we are finally on our way to the fort! Pru must have talked some sense into her mother. When we got up this morning, she told us that she had decided we must try to cross the river as soon as possible and make it to the fort before the baby comes. Yahoo!

We made it to the river again by afternoon, and I now know why they call it the Mighty Mississippi! I stood with Pru looking out at the turbulent, stormy brown waters. In the middle of the river, I could see what looked like a minitornado that Pru called a waterspout. Brush, trash, and uprooted trees floated by, as well as broken boats and rafts. The bank looked ready to crumble and fall into the river any second.

I glanced up at Mrs. Keeler sitting on the wide expanse of King George's back. She looked sick to her stomach. I hoped she wasn't getting that bug again. Her face was lined and her eyes drooped with exhaustion. She looked to me a lot like Mom did after Dad moved out. Pru was holding her mother's hand.

"Can we make it across?" I asked. "It's pretty wide here."

"I believe we should travel upriver a bit, Zoey, where there are islands in the middle of the water," Pru said.

Mrs. Keeler took a deep breath and let it out. "Mayhap we will find a ferry running. We can leave King George and ferry across to the fort."

"Leave King George! But we can't!" I said. "Who would take care of him?"

Whinny-ah-haw! King George brayed, and shook his head.

I clapped my mouth shut before more whining could escape. Mom put up with almost all the disrespect I dished out, but not Mrs. Keeler. Not even a smidgen. If or when I see Mom again, I won't smart off anymore. I'll try hard not to, anyway.

Mrs. Keeler grasped my shoulder, but not in a mean way. "I know you mean well, Zoey, but we cannot worry about a mule. We must worry about ourselves. We must get to safety before it's too late." She smiled a thin smile. "We will take King George if we can. If not, we will give the mule to another family that can use him."

Pru pulled on the reins and the mule began walking away from the river. I followed, walking by King George's side. Occasionally, I reached out to pat his shoulder. He would turn and nudge me with his nose, acknowledging my presence.

Please, God. Don't make us leave King George. I prayed the same prayer over and over. With the big animal by my side, I felt stronger—safer somehow. I knew that was probably silly. The mule was as helpless as I was to figure out what to do. But unlike the other farm animals, he hadn't run away. He had stayed. And he seemed willing to help us.

By nightfall, we had trekked farther upriver and were quite far away from Pru's home in Obion.

"I wonder if your dear papa ever reached home or if he is already at the fort," Mrs. Keeler said. Her voice cracked a bit in midsentence. Tears filled her gray eyes.

"Papa will know what to do and where to go," Pru said. "If he goes home, he will find our note and come for us."

"We'll need to stop soon and make camp," I said. "It's getting darker by the minute."

"That is a good idea," Mrs. Keeler said.

"No, Mama!" Pru said. "Let us continue on for a bit. We might see a ferry."

"I need to rest, Prudence, dear. I must get off this mule."

"But, Mama!"

"Prudence! Do not question me. We will wait for daylight."

I recognized something in Mrs. Keeler's voice, a tone that spoke of worry and fear. She didn't want to find out that there was no ferry to cross the river. Then all hope would be gone.

"It'll be all right, Pru," I said, hooking my arm through her arm and hugging it close to my side. "Let's let your mama rest." I clicked my tongue at the mule. "Whoa, boy. Time for grub."

King George stopped. Pru and I reached up to help Mrs. Keeler down. Her large belly made her bulky and hard to handle. I prayed we wouldn't drop her. When her feet touched the ground, she wobbled for a moment. I held her steady until she could stand on her own.

"If you're all right, I'll gather the wood to start the fire," I said to Mrs. Keeler. I was becoming quite the expert at wood gathering.

"Yes, you should do that before the sun drops in the sky. It is too dangerous for us to be wandering around in the dark." Mrs. Keeler waddled over to a fallen log and lowered herself down. "I will be all right here."

I took King George by the bridle and led him over to Mrs. Keeler. "Stay with her, boy," I commanded. The mule looked at me and then at Mrs. Keeler. He seemed in no hurry to disobey.

"Take the long rifle, Prudence. You might spot some game for dinner," Mrs. Keeler said. Her voice sounded weak.

"I will, Mama."

Pru and I headed into the woods. We walked in the careful, silent manner that Prudence had shown me, so as not to scare any potential game. Every few feet, I stopped to pick up branches and small logs that were the right size to use as kindling.

Pru walked with the long rifle cradled gently in her arms. She looked all around her, watching for small animals or birds. "I worry about Mama," she said in a low voice.

"I'm worried about her, too," I whispered back.

"I cannot wait to get to New Madrid," Pru said. "There will be help there. Mayhap a doctor."

I stopped in my tracks. "Did you say New Madrid?" I said, my voice unnaturally loud in the quiet woods. "I thought we were going to the fort?"

"Hush, Zoey!" Pru said. "You will scare the animals."

"But, Pru!"

"The fort is in New Madrid, Zoey. Everyone knows that. It is a nice town, bigger than Little Prairie. There are many families there. We know the Byrans and Dr. Stuart, too. Surely someone there will help poor Mama deliver the baby."

"Pru, we can't go to New Madrid!"

"Why not? If we can find a ferry to get us across the river, we will be safer there."

"New Madrid won't exist in a month or so, Pru. New Madrid is going into the river!"

Prudence

I tripped over a fallen tree at Zoey's pronouncement, making a horrible racket that certainly scared away any game. I looked at her in disbelief. "That is impossible, Zoey. I do not believe you. I am going to the fort at New Madrid!" I began to cry. "You are saying these things to scare me!"

"No, Pru, honest, I'm not. Have I been wrong yet? I'm saying these things to save you."

Zoey looked so earnest, my heart pounded in my chest. I sank to the ground. "Is this . . . is it in Mike's book?"

"Yes, Pru! I'm telling you, and you have to listen to me. We can't stay here and we can't go to the fort at New Madrid. There must be somewhere else we can go."

Zoey pulled me up, and we trudged back to Mama. I leaned for a moment against a tree and watched Zoey pacing back and forth. With her leathers on, and with her dark hair in two long braids, she did look . . . like an Indian . . . like Kalopin. What would Kalopin do?

"I think . . . I think we should continue to try to make it upriver somehow," I said after some thought. "Perhaps we can persuade a boatman to take us away from here. Not necessarily to New Madrid, but somewhere safer. Maybe we could go northeast into Kentucky."

"We tried that with the *New Orleans*, Pru. It didn't work."

"I am not speaking of a large steamboat. I am speaking of a smaller craft, owned by someone who lives in the area, someone who will take pity on dear Mama," I said.

"Someone willing to take us aboard if we separate ourselves from our money," Mama said.

"What do you mean, Mama?"

"I mean money. I have some, sewn into the lining of my petticoat. I have saved it for years. I had hoped to use it to help us purchase a new home in New Madrid. But it was also for a dire situation. This is a dire situation."

I walked over to Mama and hunkered down, looking into her tired gray eyes. "You never told me that you were saving money! And for a house!" Elation zinged through me, followed by despair. Had we had time to travel to New Madrid with Papa and get ourselves established, we might already be in a house. Now I could not foresee a time when we might have one. But, in the midst of my world gone mad, I would be happy just to have our cabin in Chickasaw Country again, whole and safe.

"I was saving it for just such a reason, Prudence. But of what use is money if we are dead? Of what use is a house here? We must get away from this infernal place, we must!" Mama began to sob.

"Yes, Mrs. Keeler, you're right," Zoey said.

"Please, Zoey, not now," I said, waving my hand back at Zoey. "Mama is upset! Can you not see that?"

Zoey walked away. I knew that I had hurt her feelings, but Mama always becomes agitated whenever Zoey begins her insistent talk about the future. I looked and saw Zoey leaning against the broad brown side of King George.

"We can use the money to get away from here, Prudence," Mama said. "We will pay someone to help us."

"Yes, Mama." I reached out to stroke Mama's cheek. "Do not fret. We will overcome."

A movement in the trees caught my attention. I rose quickly and walked over to where I had leaned the long rifle against a tree. My hands trembled a bit as I picked up the gun. I remembered the skinny man from the *New Orleans*, Turlock, with his foul mouth and shifty eyes. I swallowed hard. *Please, God. Let it be an animal.*

Another movement caught my eye, the movement of something that looked to be quite a bit taller than a squirrel, or even a deer. *A man.* Quick as a flash, I lifted the rifle to my shoulder and aimed at the trees. "I'll shoot!" I said in a loud voice.

A young man and a young woman stepped out of the woods. "Do not shoot!" the man said as he stepped in front of the woman, hands held out in front of him.

"Kalopin!" I lowered the gun and ran for my old

friend. "Kalopin! Kalopin!" I sang out. Of course he was not dead! Zoey had been mistaken. "Where have you been? Are you in good health?" My heart was pounding in my chest, and I felt flushed with happiness at seeing him again. He looked so strong and sure, and I realized why Mama so longed for Papa's help. I hoped that Kalopin would know what we should do. Perhaps he had had word from Papa, I thought as I rushed toward him.

I stopped short when I neared the two. Kalopin's companion was the dark-skinned young woman with high cheekbones and flashing eyes. Laughing Eyes. Kalopin's new wife, the daughter of Chief Copiah. I remembered her from the general store.

I will admit here that I burned with jealousy at the sight of Laughing Eyes. Why did Kalopin have to marry her? She is not even a Chickasaw squaw.

Kalopin touched his hand to the cap on his head.

"Prudence," he said. "Mistress Keeler." He looked with a good deal of curiosity at Zoey, and, of course, I can understand why. She is neither fish nor fowl, in some ways.

Mama turned her back on him and hunched down into her hide. My face flamed. Zoey stood up and approached us.

"I'm Zoey," she said, and stuck out her hand. "Zoey Smith-Jones."

No one moved, though Kalopin did touch his cap again.

"I am Kalopin. This is my wife," Kalopin said, motioning the young woman to come forward. "Her name is Laughing Eyes."

I swallowed my pride. "It is nice to see you again," I said to the young woman. "Please join us by our fire."

The young woman spoke. Her voice was soft and musical, but her tongue was foreign to us.

"'I am the daughter of Chief Copiah,' my wife says," Kalopin translated. "We married shortly before the Great Spirit rumbled across the land," he explained.

"Our best wishes to you," I said.

Zoey stared at the two of them. Mama kept her head down.

"I am happy to see that you lived through the wrath of the Great Spirit," Kalopin said to Mama, "but I fear worse is still to come. You must move north."

"Can you take us with you?" Zoey said. "I think we need to get as far away from here as possible."

Kalopin considered this question. "It is unsure yet where we will go," he said.

"I am not traveling with Indians," Mama muttered.

"Mama!" I said, embarrassed by her open animosity toward Kalopin, a young man whom Papa admires. *Papa!*

"Have you seen Papa?" I asked Kalopin. "Do you know where he is? Is he safe?"

"I am sorry, Prudence. I have not seen Reverend Keeler. If I do, would you like me to convey a message?"

"Please. Tell Papa we are safe and we hope to see him soon."

"Can't we go with you guys?" Zoey asked Kalopin again.

"I would like to help you, but I cannot risk it," Kalopin said. "We are running from Copiah. If you come with us, you might be in danger."

Kalopin's wife spoke again and then looked at him. "She asks if you are soon to birth your babe?" he translated, looking at Mama.

"Yes," I answered, since my mother seemed to have no intention of doing so. "Mama believes the baby will come in February, but she worries that it might happen sooner."

The beautiful young woman smiled and spoke again, patting her flat stomach. "'We will have a baby,'" Kalopin translated.

A baby. Kalopin had truly grown up and left me behind. I noticed that Kalopin looked at his new wife with a most tender gaze. He touched her hand, and she smiled at him. I wanted to hate Laughing Eyes, but I could not.

Zoey

(Pru says it is, anyway. I don't even know what day it is any-more. And I'm not sure I care, though I should, I guess.)

Kalopin has shown up. I've never seen Pru so happy. Or so pretty! She glows when she talks to Kalopin. She obviously has a crush on him, and I can see why. He's cute, even though he walks with a limp.

I watched from King George's side as Pru talked to her mother. Mrs. Keeler was not happy to see Kalopin and his wife again. I can tell she doesn't trust them.

Kalopin's wife was quiet. She didn't talk much, though her eyes seemed to smile at me as I was looking at her clothes. She had on a long chamois dress with lots of beadwork on it, with designs in blue, green, and yellow. It reminded me of the cover of the journal Grandma Cope made me for my birthday.

Some memory was nudging at me, but try as I might, I couldn't pull it into focus. Laughing Eyes. It was a per-fect name for her.

Kalopin was crouched down by the fire, and Laughing Eyes sat beside him. They were looking at each other, but they did not talk. I squatted near the fire the same way they did. Their clothes were so cool, especially Kalopin's outfit. It wasn't exactly what I'd expected.

Instead of long leather pants, he wore pants that only reached his knees. Around his waist he had tied a woven sash. He didn't wear a jacket but a poncho made from raccoon skins. Mrs. White from church has a raccoon jacket. Mom always sniffs in disgust whenever Mrs. White wears it.

"Do you live around here?" I asked.

"Yes. This is my country. Chickasaw Country." Kalopin turned to Laughing Eyes, who had said something to him. "My wife says to tell you she is not Chickasaw. She is Choctaw. But I say she is now Chickasaw. Chickasaw means, in our tongue, to leave. My wife had to leave her family."

"Why?" I asked.

"Laughing Eyes' father is a Choctaw chief, Chief Copiah. He did not want his daughter to marry me, even though I am a mingo. I offered him many gifts to convince him of my worthiness, but he wanted Laughing Eyes to marry a Choctaw brave. So I took her. And Chief Copiah cursed our marriage."

"I thought all the Five Civilized Tribes got along. That's what we learned in social studies."

"Laughing Eyes is a princess, destined to marry a great chief. And Copiah does not trust me since I am lame. But I could not forget her beauty. The memory of her eyes haunted me. . . ."

Suddenly, I thought of Grandma Cope and her fainting spell on Thanksgiving. What had she said to me? Something about the river and my eyes. Laughing Eyes. Yes, that was it! She called *me* Laughing Eyes! But the real Laughing Eyes was the daughter of Chief Copiah!

Why would Grandma Cope have called me that? Could she have known about Kalopin and Laughing Eyes? Could she have known that I would somehow meet them?

I looked at Kalopin. I thought about his rolling gait, and the way he limped. "Uh, Kalopin," I said, "what do they call you? In English? Do the whites have a name for you?"

Kalopin looked at me. His gaze was steady. "The white men have always called me Reelfoot."

Prudence

13 January 1812

Kalopin and Laughing Eyes are still with us. Laughing Eyes is with child, though not far along. I expect that she will have a baby by late summer. Earlier, we talked about what Zoey claims to know, and what Kalopin believes will happen to him. It was an extraordinary conversation. I will record it here.

We all squatted around the fire except Mama and Laughing Eyes. Mama was lying on some skin robes. Laughing Eyes sat by her side, watching. At first, Mama had objected to the young woman's presence, but as the afternoon wore on, she accepted it. Occasionally, Laughing Eyes would wet a rag and wipe Mama's face and neck. For all that it was cold, Mama was sweating. Her pains had begun again, too. I worried about her, but I turned my attention back to Kalopin and Zoey in order to hear them better.

"You say that there will be a great flood?" Kalopin was asking Zoey.

"Yes. When the earthquake hits, all of what you call Chickasaw Country will be underwater. A lake will form. Not a deep one, but a big one."

"Zoey has told me this story before, Kalopin," I said.

"And you say this lake will bear my name?" Kalopin asked.

"Yes. People will call it Reelfoot Lake, after you," Zoey said.

Kalopin was quiet for a while. "Then it is true. . . ." He was silent another moment. "You must get out of Chickasaw Country," he said, looking at me. "You must leave before this great flood occurs."

"Finally, someone believes me!" Zoey said.

Kalopin nodded. "The Great Spirit warned me that if I stole Laughing Eyes away from Chief Copiah, the earth would rock and the waters would swallow up my village and bury my people in a watery grave."

Kalopin looked over at Laughing Eyes.

"Didn't you believe him?" Zoey said. "I mean, him being the Great Spirit and all?"

"I wanted Laughing Eyes for my bride. And she grew to love me while I visited her village last spring."

"So that's when you stole her?" Zoey asked.

I sat still, trying to absorb the things I had heard.

"No, not then. I swallowed my longing for Laughing Eyes and returned north to Chickasaw Country. But when the maize was gathered, I could no longer bear to live apart from my love. So I ignored the Great Spirit's warnings and returned south. Under cover of night, I stole my bride."

"And that's when the earthquakes started?" Zoey asked.

"Yes, the rumblings began. That is why I believe your story. Also, I had a vision." He looked at me. "I saw Zoey in my vision. I did not know who she was but believed her to be a Chickasaw."

"But I'm only part Chickasaw. My grandma Cope is Chickasaw and Choctaw," Zoey said. Then a complete look of puzzlement came over her face.

Kalopin nodded. "Yes, Chief Copiah and Laughing Eyes are Choctaw."

"I said Cope," Zoey said, her eyes wild. "Not Copiah. Cope!"

"You are part of my destiny, Zoey," Kalopin said. "You and your grandma Copiah. That is why you have come back to be with us. Your destiny is to save your people."

Kalopin was looking at Zoey. For once, I could see that Zoey was speechless.

With all my being, I want this nightmare to end. I want to wake up by the fire, with dear Papa having his breakfast and reading his Bible nearby. I want never to feel the ground roll beneath my feet again. I want never to smell the horrible odors that erupt out of gashes in the dirt, spewing sand and water and sometimes a noxious black liquid up and over my feet. I gladly would give up having met Zoey if my world would stop shaking and shifting beneath my feet—if Papa were home and Mama were well and the baby could be born—and live—in safety.

I felt sick and jumped up. My stomach heaved. I turned away from the fire in time. What little I have eaten recently came up, burning my throat. My stomach was becoming as weak as Zoey's!

"You must not fear Copiah's curse. It is my destiny," Kalopin said. "In my vision, I saw her," he said again, pointing at Zoey. "I believed at first she was a Chickasaw, and then it seemed she was a Choctaw. Finally, the Great Spirit showed me that she is both—Chickasaw and Choctaw."

For the first time that I can remember since she arrived here, Zoey looked proud upon hearing that she is part Indian. She nodded at Kalopin in what looked to be agreement.

"But aren't you going to try and get away?" Zoey asked. "Save yourself? And Laughing Eyes and your child that is on its way?"

"I do not believe I can," Kalopin said. "It may be too late."

"But shouldn't you try?" Zoey cried. "I mean, it seems to me that you have to. Because . . . because that must be why I'm here. My Grandma Cope is your descendant!" Zoey shook her head, looking amazed. "I'm related to Laughing Eyes—and to you. You have to save yourself!"

Kalopin shook his head. "It is not my destiny to live through the wrath of the Great Spirit."

"What about your vision? Of me, and the future?" Zoey asked.

"I do not know yet. I must think on these things," Kalopin said. He walked away from us and Laughing Eyes followed him.

"Don't cry, Pru," Zoey said.

I reached up and touched my cheeks. They were wet with tears. I had not realized I was crying.

"Reelfoot knows his own destiny. I know it's terrible, but he's right," she said. "He will drown in the flood, and the lake will be named for him. At least, that's what the legend says." Zoey sniffled. "But if he saves Laughing Eyes, then my Grandma Cope will be born someday."

"Please, Zoey, enough!" I said. "Maybe your tale is only that—a legend. Maybe Kalopin does not have to die."

"I wish that was so, Pru," Zoey said, "but I think it was my destiny to come back in time and meet Reelfoot and set right the wrong he did Copiah. He is supposed to save Laughing Eyes, and I'm here to make sure it happens. So that my own family will survive. And yours, too." She wiped her eyes on her sleeve.

I could see that Zoey did not want to upset me. I could see that she was uneasy about her realizations. But I feared they were true.

Kalopin returned to where we sat. "We must move north, toward the fort. The white men there can help you."

"Zoey believes New Madrid will soon fall into the river, Kalopin," I told him. Zoey nodded at us.

"Not west, as the sun falls, but north. If the fort at New Madrid is to fall into the river, the soldiers will move to the north, to the fort in Kentucky they call Jefferson."

"You are right, Kalopin," I agreed. "We can attempt to make it into Kentucky."

"What about me?" Zoey asked.

"You will come with us, of course," I replied.

"But how will I ever get home to my own time"—Zoey took a deep gulping breath—"if I am not where I was when I got here?"

Zoey

We're on the road again, heading north into Kentucky with Reelfoot and Laughing Eyes. By noon, we had slowed down, so I clicked my tongue at King George. "Giddap, you big brute!" I said as I pulled on his rein. King George butted his head into my back, but he picked up the pace a bit. I reached out and patted him.

Mrs. Keeler was no longer on his back. Before we began our journey, Reelfoot helped us build a kind of travois to pull Mrs. Keeler, who is finding it more and more difficult to walk and even to sit up. In the last few days, she has ballooned, it looks like, and can hardly get around.

Reelfoot tied two heavy ropes between two long poles and then attached the poles on either side of King George. George was pulling Mrs. Keeler. It was a bumpy ride at times, but she assured us that it was easier than trying to walk.

"I think Kalopin plans to leave us soon," Pru said at my side.

A little shiver of fear went up my spine. I didn't want Reelfoot to leave us yet. All the talk about destinies, curses, Grandma Cope, Chief Copiah, and the Great Spirit had spooked me. I wanted Reelfoot to stay close and run interference for me with the Great Spirit.

"He has been whispering to Laughing Eyes for some time now. He has given her his fur robe."

"Maybe she's cold."

"I think he plans to meet his destiny like a proud Indian brave," Pru said. "I think he plans to return to Chickasaw Country."

"Maybe. I wish I could know what's the right thing for all of us to do. It's so confusing! For now, though, we need to be worrying about your mama," I said. "I think she's going to go into labor any time now."

Pru turned white. "Why do you think that? Has she said anything?"

"To me? Ha! No. But she's moaning and groaning. I think her pains have started again."

"What must we do?"

"We need to hurry and get someplace flat and solid, near some water, where we can build a fire and get ready," I answered. "And soon."

We plodded along for another mile; then we let King George take the lead and walked back to see how Mrs. Keeler was doing.

"I believe your Kalopin is a decent man."

"He is, Mama. I have always known it. But what makes you believe now?" Prudence asked.

"I have been watching him with his wife," Mrs. Keeler said. "He cares for her. He is gentle with her."

"Yes, Mama," Pru said, "he is."

I noticed that she sounded sad, or maybe resigned. She cared a lot more about Reelfoot than I ever did about Robbie. "Don't be sad, Pru," I said. "You'll meet a great guy someday and probably get married and have tons of kids!"

"I do not know, Zoey, but I hope that will come to pass. It is a lonely, hard life for a woman without a man."

I thought about Mom and tears sprang to my eyes. I wonder if she and Dad have worked through any of their problems. I wonder if my disappearance has brought them closer together or driven them further apart. I wonder if all their arguing about career paths and dreams and fulfillment means anything to them now.

January 19

(Pru says it is a Sunday. I guess I have to believe her.)

The baby is coming—*today!* Mrs. Keeler finally admitted to me that she's in full labor now, with pains a couple of minutes apart. I wish Mom was here! She would help us feel calm and natural about the whole thing, instead of being nervous wrecks, like we all obviously are.

"What the heck should we do?" I said. "How can we help you, Grace?"

"I *have* had babies, remember?" Mrs. Keeler smiled a

weak smile at me. "I will tell you when it is time. And you *may* call me Grace."

I smiled. It would be easier to call her Grace. Maybe she liked me a little bit.

All morning long, I listened to Grace moaning and crying out. Her face was a sickly yellow color and slicked with sweat. Her dress was soaked beneath her. Her yellow hair lay in lank strands across her shoulders. Her eyes were sunken, with dark circles around them. Her lips were pale, with a bluish tinge.

None of the women I had ever seen in labor under my mother's watch had looked as bad as Grace—so bone weary and sick.

Reelfoot kept his distance, but once, when we were coming back from the creek with fresh water, Laughing Eyes was washing Grace's face. Grace was either beginning to trust Reelfoot and Laughing Eyes a bit more, or she was in too much pain to protest.

"I fear Mama will die, or the baby, or both," Pru said from behind me, voicing my fears and making me even more scared. "What will I do?"

I turned and saw how frightened Pru looked. I couldn't blame her. If Grace died and the baby lived, then Pru and I would have to figure out how to care for the baby in the middle of nowhere. If both Grace *and* the baby died, where would we go? Would we ever find our way to civilization? Who would take care of us?

Prudence

Mama will have the baby soon, or die in the attempt. It is imminent, she says. Kalopin has left us to go and check our traps and do some hunting, as we are out of fresh game. I think he might want to let Mama have some privacy, too. Laughing Eyes has stayed behind. I hope to convince Mama to let her help us.

"Boil water, Pru, and tear some clean cloths into rags," Zoey said from where she squatted in front of Mama. "They always boil water on TV," she mumbled to herself.

"Yes, Zoey," I answered. I hurried to do as Zoey bid, but the cloths would have to come from my petticoat, I supposed, and I did not know how clean that might be.

When the water was hot, Zoey pushed her hands into the pot and washed them quickly with the lye soap we had brought with us from home, and then instructed me to do the same. Then she rinsed out some of the cloths in the hot water.

"Boil some fresh water, Pru," she said. "And drop a sharp knife down into the pot to boil it clean, but leave the handle sticking out, or it will be too hot when we need it. That's what they do on TV." Then she strode over to Mama and knelt down.

"The baby is coming!" Mama cried.

I rushed from the fire to be near her. "Mama, let Laughing Eyes help, please!" I pleaded with her.

"Yes, yes, ask her to help me," she said between clenched teeth. "Please!"

I ran to get Laughing Eyes and when I returned, Zoey seemed to have the situation well in hand, but she moved aside to let Laughing Eyes look, too.

"Is it time?" Zoey asked her. She made believe she was rocking a baby, then pointed at Mama and nodded vigorously. Laughing Eyes nodded as well.

Laughing Eyes settled on the ground beside Zoey and encouraged Mama to push.

At first, nothing seemed to be happening, but then everything happened very fast and before I knew it, I saw the top of the baby's head, and then a little wrinkled face. Zoey leaned over Laughing Eyes and wiped the baby's face with a clean, wet cloth. Miraculously, the baby opened its mouth and mewled. Its little face crumpled and it grimaced.

"The baby is alive! Praise God!" Mama cried and laughed at the same time.

Zoey looked up at me, her mouth a wide O of surprise. Then she looked down at the living creature she had helped birth and burst into tears. I began to cry as well. Laughing Eyes smiled her bright smile.

The baby opened his little mouth and wailed, screwing up his entire face and turning beet red.

Zoey laughed. "It's a boy, Grace. You have a baby boy!"

My heart was about to burst, I was so excited, and Zoey looked as excited as I felt.

"Oh, Zoey, look at him! He is beautiful," I said.

While Laughing Eyes was helping Mama, I examined my new brother. He was small, but he was breathing.

Zoey shook her head. "Never in a million years would I have imagined that I would be holding a newborn baby in my hands—a baby that I helped to bring into the world! And I didn't throw up or anything! My mom would be so proud of me!" Zoey quickly wiped her eyes.

When Laughing Eyes was done, Zoey handed the baby to me. "You've got to keep the baby warm, Pru. If he catches a chill, it'll be dangerous. Put him inside your dress and then wrap one of those skins around you."

I hesitated for only a second.

"Go on, Pru, give him your body heat!" Zoey watched me as I sat down near Mama with the baby wrapped inside my dress. We did it! We helped Mama deliver her baby.

Zoey turned back to Mama. "It should all be over soon, Grace," she said. "Just a little longer."

Zoey

I looked at Grace. She was pale and still. I wondered what Mom would do. A memory of the night I saw the comet at Mambo Taco came back to me, Norah talking about massaging a woman's stomach after a baby comes. I snapped my fingers. "I'm going to massage your belly. That will help things along. Is that all right?" I asked Grace.

"Yes, Zoey, if you must," Grace whispered.

The baby was making loud crying sounds, interspersed with howling, and broken up by squalling, as Pru tried to get him situated. Grace looked over at the two of them. She smiled a little.

I placed my hands flat on Grace's belly and began to rub firmly. "Hmm. Mom always said the belly should be soft," I said to Grace. "But yours feels hard."

Grace looked alarmed.

"I'm sure it's okay," I said, but I wondered. I wished I'd listened more closely to Mom and her friends and all that talk at Mambo Taco. What had Grandma Cope told me? *Pay attention, Zoey!*

I turned to Laughing Eyes, who had stepped away from Grace after the baby was born. "What do you think, Laughing Eyes?" I said, pointing at Grace's belly and making rubbing motions.

Laughing Eyes came closer and knelt down by Grace. She hesitated for a moment, but when Grace nodded, she reached down and rubbed Grace's belly, too.

"What is it?" I said.

Laughing Eyes smiled at me and then made the baby-rocking motion with her arms.

"I know she had a baby, but what now?" I asked. I felt a little frustrated—and scared. I wished Mom would magically appear and take over.

Laughing Eyes pointed to Grace's belly and made the rubbing motion.

Grace reached down and rubbed her own belly. "You are right, Zoey, my belly should be soft and it is not," Grace said.

"Do you think there's a problem? What should I do?"

"I do not think there is a problem, Zoey, dear," Grace said with a little smile. "I think we have another baby to birth."

Prudence

I held my brother close to my heart, beneath my dress, against my skin. He had stopped crying. He seemed to be gazing around, but I wondered how much he could see, if anything. Could he tell how much I loved him already? My heart expanded with the thought that this child, after all that Mama and I have endured, had made it safely into the world. And another baby was coming!

Will Papa ever see this child, his son? Where could Papa be? Is he looking for us?

Mama moaned, drawing my attention. I hurried over to where Zoey and Laughing Eyes attended to her, holding the baby so as not to jostle him. "Is it happening, Mama? Is the other baby coming?"

Mama gritted her teeth. "Yes!" Mama cried out with pain. "Oh my good Lord!"

"It'll be over soon, Grace," Zoey said. "Hold on a little longer."

Zoey handed me the knife. "Go put that back in the small pot, Pru. We're going to need it again soon."

I wiped the knife off with a cloth and then placed it in the pot with the handle up. I looked over at poor Mama and blushed. I cannot remember ever having seen my mother's bare legs.

Zoey was a little green, but she was calm. She was wiping Mama's face with a cloth and talking to her in a low voice. I wondered what she was saying to her.

Laughing Eyes sat on the quilt in front of Mama. She waited quietly.

"Pru, bring another quilt over to put the next baby in. It's coming soon," Zoey called.

When I got to Zoey's side, Mama screamed. I looked. And just as before, without warning, there was another baby! "It's a girl, Mama! A girl! I have a sister," I said, and began to cry. With a quick intake of breath, the new baby joined me, wailing in a loud voice.

After Laughing Eyes cut the cord, she wrapped the baby in the quilt and handed her to Mama, who cuddled her close.

"Now we have to massage your belly again, Grace," Zoey said to Mama. "Hey, you don't think you've got any other little Keelers hiding in there, do you?"

"Zoey!" I said in shock. What a thing to say, and especially to my proper mother!

"It is a joke, Prudence, dear," Mama said with a weak smile, surprising me. "No, Zoey, I believe that these two babies are all the Keelers that are coming today," she continued. "And that was one more than I was expecting."

I grinned and hugged my brother close. A brother! A sister! And a girl like Zoey for a friend.

Though the earthquakes destroyed my home, and Mama and I are far from any neighbors or doctors, I do not feel frightened. Two miracles have occurred in my life. Three if I count Zoey. I prayed for a friend. I prayed for a healthy baby brother or sister. My prayers have been answered. Now if only dear Papa would return to us.

Zoey

The morning after the babies were born, we woke up and Reelfoot and Laughing Eyes had disappeared. We talked about what to do and decided to continue moving north, as we'd been doing when they were with us. But I could tell that Grace was upset. She didn't want to talk about Reelfoot or Laughing Eyes and frowned at us whenever their names came up.

I had a bad feeling about today from the moment I woke up. I was snoozing away, half-dead from all the excitement of the last few days—and the hourly squalling of the hungry babies—when a rumbling sound burrowed its way into my consciousness. A thundering, rumbling noise that sounded like . . .

"Earthquake!" I mumbled as I sat up and tried to disentangle myself from the pile of quilts and rugs on top of me. I stopped when I noticed Pru and Grace sitting by the fire, the babies in their arms. They were looking at something behind me. I turned my head and saw a herd of deer running through the woods. They weren't thrashing about in terror the way they had during the first quake, but they were definitely leaving the area.

"It is starting again, is it not?" Pru called across to me. "More quakes?" Her voice sounded resigned.

"Yes, Pru, I think so," I said.

Pru and Grace made no move to get up.

"When I went to the creek for water this morning, there were fish jumping out of the water onto the creek bank," Grace said. "Just as before—before the first time."

I jumped up and hurried to the fire. "Shouldn't we try to get prepared somehow? Do something?"

"What *can* we do, Zoey?" Pru said. She looked tired. Her hair, usually neatly combed and braided, was down and its long reddish blond length was tangled and matted. Pru's face was smudged, too, and her dress was dirty and torn.

I felt guilty. Pru had been awake almost continuously since the birth of the babies, helping her mother take care of them. When one was eating, the other was wailing, waiting to eat. I *knew* Grace had to be tired. She didn't even turn away from me or attempt to cover herself to nurse the babies the way she had the first day.

Suddenly, the air roared and whistled around us as the intensity of the earthquake forced the ground to open in long fissures. Fumes seeped out of the earth and the sky turned dark. The heavy, rotten-egg smell assaulted my nose. I buried my face in Pru's hair to escape it, but it didn't help.

Whinny-ah-haw! King George screamed, and with one powerful jerk, the big animal pulled away from the tree where we had tied him the night before and bolted.

"George!" I shouted. "George!"

Beside me, Grace prayed. I didn't recognize the words, but it was comforting, so I mumbled along with them. "Forever and ever, amen," I joined in at the end. "And God, please watch over King George," I added.

"Please watch over us!" Grace amended.

"Yeah, us, too," I whispered. But my heart was aching for George. I hoped the mule would not break a leg or worse on the unstable ground.

"We must move. The earth ahead is sinking," Grace declared. We stood up and helped Grace to her feet. "This way," she said, and motioned us in an easterly direction.

I looked to my left as we hurried away from the sinkhole. Black liquid oozed up out of the ground, filling the hole. The ground still trembled beneath us. Trees were splitting and falling by the dozens in the densely wooded area in the distance.

I felt like I was in the middle of a war movie.

After we were well away from the sinkhole, we continued to walk east. Eventually, the rumbling subsided a bit, but an occasional aftershock caused us to stumble in our tracks. Still we kept moving.

Around sunset, we stopped to make a fire and eat. The aftershocks hadn't stopped completely. "We should keep moving," I told Grace and Pru as we ate. "North, like Reelfoot said. Maybe we'll meet up with some other folks." I really wanted to meet up with some other folks. I hadn't realized how scary it was going it alone until Reelfoot and Laughing Eyes left us. "We need to find those Creeks—"

"Yes. We must get to higher ground," a deep voice interrupted. I looked up. Reelfoot stepped out of the woods. Alone.

Prudence

Kalopin has returned. Alone. We are on the move.

"Where did you go when you left us?" I asked my friend, hugging my sister close to me. "And where is Laughing Eyes?"

"I returned Laughing Eyes to her father, Chief Copiah. Perhaps she will escape the curse."

"Why did you come back?" Mama said. She walked along, holding my baby brother. I knew that my mother was not happy to see Kalopin again. She did not trust him now.

"Didn't you want to stay with Laughing Eyes? And maybe save yourself?" Zoey asked.

"It is not safe for Laughing Eyes to stay with me. My fate is in the hands of the Great Spirit. Your fate as well, Zoey," Kalopin said.

"My fate? What do you mean?" Zoey asked. "Maybe my fate is just to stay with Pru and help her and her mother."

167

Kalopin ignored this. "The Great Spirit came to me in another vision. You will not be with Prudence for many more days. I returned to help you meet your fate."

"I don't know if I like the sound of that," Zoey said. "I don't really know the Great Spirit all that well."

"Do not talk like that, Kalopin!" I said. "You are frightening Zoey." He was frightening me, too!

"I'm not scared," Zoey said, but I knew she had lost some of her faith in Kalopin when he left us.

Kalopin looked at Zoey and then at me. His dark eyes were compassionate. "There is no need for fear."

"Easy for you to say," Zoey said. She strode ahead of us to walk along with Mama.

"Kalopin, what do you mean when you say that Zoey must meet her fate?" I said when she was out of earshot.

"Zoey's destiny is not here, in this place or this time. Yours is, and that of your family. But not mine. Nor hers."

"What about Laughing Eyes? Did she not ask you to stay with her?" I asked. I no longer felt jealous of Laughing Eyes. I wished that she had been able to talk Kalopin out of this nonsense about destiny.

"A brave must meet his fate. But a brave must also perform his duties. I returned Laughing Eyes to Copiah. My child will be born. Copiah will raise him to be a chief, a Choctaw chief. My wife will live to marry again. It is her time."

The baby in my arms began to mew its hungry cry. "Baby girl is hungry, Mama. Is my brother finished?" Mama still had not named the babies. I knew she hoped that Papa would find us soon and help her. But she might be thinking about it. Just this morning, she had asked me about Zoey's full name.

"Yes," Mama said. We stopped walking so that Mama and I could trade babies. When Mama handed my brother to me, I sniffed his sweet head and then tucked him under my cloak before he became chilled.

Mama took the baby Zoey had been holding for her.

"What will happen to Zoey?" I said.

"Her fate is in the hands of the Great Spirit. She must not run from it. She will have to be courageous." Kalopin's eyes shone with a strange light. "The river will come for us," he said.

I shivered and held my brother closer.

We walked along in silence for another hour, heading north, always north. We stayed in the open, away from the trees. At times, tremors shook the ground beneath our feet, but we had become so used to it that we continued to plod along.

2 February 1812

Kalopin led us to a Creek village north of Chickasaw Country. He is a cousin to the wife of the chief of this village. He has warned them that they must move north and east, away from the area. We will travel with them.

I sat with Zoey and some of the young Indian maidens. The girls were roasting fish that they had caught that morning with nets. My stomach grumbled.

Mama sat across the fire with the older women. When we first arrived in the village a week ago, Mama acted stiff and reserved around the Creeks. She did not want to stay in the village with them. When the women crowded around, clicking their tongues, smiling, and showing their enthusiasm over the twins, she grew a bit friendlier. Now she even lets the women hold the babies and help her bathe them.

I am happy to be among people, even these Indians who cannot, for the most part, speak English. Zoey and I bathed and washed our clothes in the creek. Unfortunately, most of what we carried along with us disappeared with King George. Zoey still has her backpack with a few items in it, but she has lost her leathers. She wears an old dress of mine, and a bonnet, too. I think she looks quite lovely. Zoey has pronounced herself hideous.

Kalopin stepped away from the group of men who had been talking and approached the fire. "We must talk," he said, pointing to me and Zoey.

We stood up. A few of the Indian girls giggled behind their hands. I blushed. I hoped they did not think anything was improper in our friendship with Kalopin.

"When the sun rises, the tribe will leave on its journey north. You"—he pointed at me—"will go with them, along with your mother and the babies. You"—he pointed at Zoey—"will come with me."

Zoey

No matter how hard I try to convince Reelfoot that I need to go north with Pru and Grace and the babies, he insists that I must go with him. Of course, he can't make me, but he seems so sure. He talks about the Great Spirit having a plan for me. Well, the Great Spirit has *some* kind of plan for me, and maybe it is to spend the rest of my life in the olden days with Pru and her family. Gosh knows they could use my help!

But I want to go home to Mom and Dad. And Grandma Cope! For now, though, I'm still here.

Pru and I sat near the fire, changing the babies' diapers, or clouts, as Pru calls them, since they aren't diapers at all, but clean rags that we tie around them. Of course, now they were dirty rags. I remember babysitting for my neighbor and changing little Anthony's disposable diaper. I thought that was so gross at the time. But that was a snap compared to this mess.

"Do we wash these out?" I asked Pru, holding up one of the cloths.

"No, not if they are only wet," Pru answered. "We dry them and reuse them."

I opened my mouth to express my disgust but clapped it shut before the words could burst forth. With no washing machine in sight, of course we would have to reuse the clouts.

I bundled the baby girl back into her blanket. "What should I do, Pru? What do you think?" Pru and I had been talking nonstop about my situation with the Great Spirit. I tried to joke about it, but I was scared to death.

"I do not know, Zoey. I do not want you to leave us, but that is for purely selfish reasons. You must do what you think is right."

"Do you trust Reelfoot—Kalopin?" I asked her.

"I know him. He is honest." Pru looked at me. Her round blue eyes brimmed with tears. "I do trust him. But . . . I fear if you leave with him, I will never see the two of you again."

I took Pru's rough hand in mine. "I'm afraid of that, too," I said. "I don't know what to do. I'm scared to go north and scared to go with Reelfoot. I wish someone would send me a sign. If I go, then tonight is my last night with you and your mom and the babies, maybe forever."

"I know," Pru said. She was crying hard now.

"Don't cry, Pru! It'll be all right. I'll figure it out." I picked up the baby girl. "These babies need names, you know, Pru," I said, in an effort to change the subject. "We can't keep calling them baby girl and baby boy forever."

Pru sniffled. "You are right. Mama is thinking about it."

We settled down on our pallets, each with a baby cuddled up next to our bodies to help warm them. That way, Grace could get some rest between feedings.

"Good night, Zoey," Pru said. "Sleep well."

The ground shook and a cloud of vapor blurred my vision. I could not see Pru and Grace. Where were they? I would be lost if I didn't catch up with them soon.

"Pru! Grace!" I called. "Where are you?"

I peered into the fog. King George! Was that King George? I ran toward the mule and tripped over a fallen tree. I heard the creaking of splintered branches above me and scrambled to my feet, moving just in time to escape the crash of a heavy limb on my head.

"Zoey! Zoey! It is time to leave," a woman's voice called.

The voice sounded familiar, and I whipped around to see who was speaking. No one. Only the vaporous mist on all sides.

"Zoey, it is time for you to face your destiny."

The air stilled. For a moment, I wasn't sure what was happening, but then it occurred to me that the screeching of animals and creaking of trees had stopped.

"I'm scared," I whispered.

"Be strong. Follow Reelfoot. Face your destiny."

"But what if I don't make it back?"

"Be strong. Trust."

"Trust in what?"

"Trust in yourself. Everything is unfolding as it should. Follow Reelfoot to face your destiny."

I felt water rising around my ankles, cold rushing water. Water that smelled of fish and mud . . .

"Trust the river. A river will never lie to you."

I woke up in the growing light of dawn. It was time to go. Grandma Cope had said so.

Prudence

The earth never stopped moving today. Zoey and Kalopin took leave of us. Even Mama cried.

"Zoey, Mama wants to have a word with you before you go," I told my friend as she was packing her bag with pemmican in preparation for the return trip south to Obion. I know Zoey does not like the dried meat, but it is good on a journey.

"Okay, Pru." Zoey left her packing and walked over to where Mama sat with the other women and the babies. I followed, curious to know what my mother wanted to discuss with Zoey.

"You wanted to talk to me, Grace?" Zoey asked.

"Yes. Sit down, Zoey."

Zoey sat beside Mama. She reached over to stroke the downy blond hair on the baby girl's head. She tickled the other baby under his chin.

"Prudence told me your given name, but I want to make certain of it," Mama said. "Would you say it for me?"

"It's weird," Zoey answered.

"Tell me, please."

"Okay. I mean, yes, ma'am. It's Zoey Saffron Lennon Smith-Jones. I'd rather just be Zoey Jones, to tell you the truth." Zoey sighed. "I have to admit, some things about the old days weren't too bad. Things seem so much simpler here."

"I do not always understand what you are saying, Zoey," Mama said. "But before you take leave of us, I would like you to know that I have decided on names for the babies."

"You have? What did you pick?"

"I will call my new daughter Saffron Keeler. I will call my new son Lennon Keeler. In honor of you, Zoey, who helped bring them safely into the world." Mama smiled at Zoey, the first full and genuine smile I had seen on my mother's face in months.

I looked to see how Zoey was taking this news. My friend's face had turned red and tears streamed down her cheeks, but she was silent. After a moment, she sniffled hard and wiped her eyes with the back of her hand. "Gosh, Grace. I don't think I've ever felt so honored. Or humbled. In my whole life."

"If we do not meet again, Zoey, I will not soon forget you. I doubt I ever could. If I have been less than kind, please forgive me. The last few months were an uncertain time for us, and we face an uncertain future." Mama took Zoey's hand in hers and held it. My heart felt full. It pleased me so to see Mama looking at Zoey with affection.

"It's no problem, Grace. You've had a lot of stress on you. I understand," Zoey said to Mama.

"I will miss you, Zoey," I said. I reached over and took her other hand. "We both will miss you, won't we, Mama?"

"Yes. Knowing you has been . . . well, I have no words for it." Mama smiled at us.

"It's been pretty wild for me, too, Grace," Zoey said with a laugh. She reached over and hugged Mama. I saw Mama stiffen for a moment, unused to such displays of affection, but then she relented and hugged Zoey back. She rubbed her cheek against Zoey's before letting her go.

"I have something for you, Grace," Zoey said, reaching into the pocket of her dress. She handed Mama a small, flat object.

On one side was a painting of four men wearing strange-looking blue suits. They all had clean-shaven faces and big smiles. Mama turned it over. "And what am I to do with this?" she said after examining it.

"Look at yourself," Zoey said. "That was my mom's mirror. She loved the Beatles. They were a cool band back in the sixties. Or should I say *ahead* in the sixties? They played some great rock-and-roll music."

"Mayhap you should keep this mirror to give back to your mother?" Mama looked at Zoey with a soft expression.

Zoey considered this. "I think she would want me to give it to you, Grace. If I ever get home, Mom won't care a thing about that mirror. And neither will I." Her eyes were shiny with tears.

"I will treasure it all my life as a memory of our friend Zoey," Mama said.

We stood up and walked back to where Zoey had been packing. "If I don't get back to my own time, or things don't happen the way they're supposed to, Pru, I'll be back." Zoey's eyes had tears in them still, though she was not crying.

"Are you certain you should go?" I asked. I was not as convinced about the plan as Zoey seemed to be.

"Yes," she said with a little smile. She took my hand in hers. "Yes. It's time."

"But it was a dream, Zoey. Dreams do not mean anything." I hoped that this did not hurt her feelings, but Papa and Mama had never set much store on signs and prognostications.

"Pru, I don't know if it was a sign or just a dream. But what else do I have to go on? I feel like I have this one chance to get back to my parents and my own time. It may not work out. I might end up more lost than ever. But I have to try. Isn't it worth it?"

"I am frightened, Zoey," I said. "What will we do without you?"

"Don't be afraid, Pru. You'll be all right."

Zoey's face was serene, much like Kalopin's.

"Mayhap we should plan to meet in the future, if you do not make it back?" I ventured.

Zoey's lips curved. "The future? As in *my* future? Do you have something planned that I don't know about, Pru?" she asked.

I realized what I had said, and laughed as well. "I mean the immediate future, of course. I am certain I would never survive in your future."

"Oh, I don't know. You're smart and you've got excellent manners. That goes a long way anywhere or anytime," Zoey said. "And you're pretty, too!"

I felt myself blush. No one had ever told me I was pretty as many times as Zoey. "You remind me of my friend Lizzie Bryan," I told Zoey. "She is impulsive and says things I never could, and she is so jolly to be around."

"I hope you get to hang out with Lizzie again soon." Zoey touched my arm.

"Lizzie lives in New Madrid. I pray she and her family are safe," I said.

"I'll pray for them, too." Zoey's lips trembled a bit.

"Mama says that after we go north with the Indians, we will stay in Kentucky, possibly at Fort Jefferson, until the weather is warmer, maybe March. Then we will try to go back to the fort at New Madrid, if it is still standing. She wants to find out if Papa has been seen or heard from, or if there is any mail from him for us there. If you don't make it home, will you try to find your way to New Madrid?"

Zoey's eyes lit up. "That's a brilliant idea. But how?"

"Cross the river into the Louisiana Territory. Ask any folks you see. A ferry crosses over and lands close to the fort. We will try to leave word for you, if we do not find you there already." I tried to sound reassuring, but it was all so uncertain.

"I'll do the same, Pru. I promise. And if there is no word from me, just assume that I made it back. Don't think anything bad or worry about me." Zoey smiled her brilliant smile, but her lips were trembling again.

"It will be hard not to," I said. "I will pray for your safety."

"Listen, Pru. Tell Saffron and Lennon about me," Zoey said.

"Yes! I will write about you in my journal, and I will tell my children about my good friend Zoey, and how you saved us." I sighed. "If I ever get married and have children, that is."

"You will, Pru! Some guy is going to snap you up, just wait and see!"

I smiled. "With any luck, my world will right itself soon, and I will be able to return to school. For now, my duty is to Mama. I must help with Saffron and Lennon."

Zoey laughed. "Those names don't sound so bad to me anymore," she said.

Zoey

February 4, Tuesday

I can't believe I'm trekking through the countryside alone. Well, I might as well be alone. Reelfoot's the strong, silent type, I guess, and he hasn't said more than a few words since we left Pru and Grace. If Mom and Dad knew I was wandering around in the middle of nowhere with a stranger, they would freak!

But times are different now, or here, I should say. I trust Reelfoot. Even though years and years separate us, I feel connected to him, which is a crazy thought—but no crazier than anything else I've been through lately, I guess.

"Where are we going, exactly?" I asked Reelfoot when we stopped to rest.

"We will return to Chickasaw Country," Reelfoot said. "I must return to our people."

I pondered for a moment. "Are we going to be okay? I don't want us to die. I'm really afraid of dying."

Reelfoot looked at me. His gaze was steady and sure.

181

"Do not be afraid of death. It is only a journey to some-where else."

"I *am* afraid. I can't help it." I felt a little ashamed to admit that, but at least I didn't sound whiny about it, which was an improvement. "And you sound like my Grandma Cope. Everything's a journey to her."

Reelfoot smiled a bit at that. "Why did you follow me, Zoey?" he asked.

"I heard a voice. It was Grandma Cope. She told me to follow you to my destiny. Her voice told me to trust the river."

"To have a dream is a good sign," Reelfoot said. "Many times, it is from dreams that we gain our spiritual power. Dreams give us guidance."

We were quiet a moment. I chewed pemmican. It tasted like shoe leather, but I was happy to have some-thing to eat.

"Did your dream reveal your death?" Reelfoot said.

"No, thankfully. Do you still believe you will die?" I didn't want to hear his answer, but I needed to know where things stood.

"Yes. I plan to meet my death face to face. I will not run from it."

"But you took Laughing Eyes home, right? To save her?"

"Yes. I hope Laughing Eyes lives, and my child. That is my pride." Reelfoot looked off into the distance. "But I will not test fate by trying to save myself. I hope the Great Spirit will be satisfied."

"What's the plan? I mean, what are we doing?"

"We go to Chickasaw Country, the area that you said will be a great body of water soon. We wait." Reelfoot stood. "I will try to convince my tribe to leave."

"Maybe nothing will happen," I said. "Maybe it's not your time to die yet. Or mine."

Reelfoot began walking south. "I am certain."

I hurried after him. What choice did I have?

Reelfoot is my kin—my family. If I don't go with him, I may never live in the future. I'll never know Grandma Cope, because she won't live, either. I've got to get back to her—back to my whole family in the future.

February 5, Wednesday

We made it to Chickasaw Country. I'll say this: I'm in great shape now! I've never walked so much in my life. I bet I can make the track team when I get home. If I get home.

When we got to the village, no one seemed surprised when their young chief showed up with me at his side. The Chickasaws are gentle, friendly people. They offered me food and a pallet to sleep on. The women helped me bathe, and wash my clothes, which were getting really dirty. It wasn't so much fun, though, not being able to talk to anyone. Reelfoot is one of about three men here who speak more than a few words of English. None of the women speak any.

I saw many deer symbols, and Reelfoot explained

that his tribe is the white deer clan. The white deer is their guardian and spirit guide.

"We do not eat the white deer," Reelfoot said.

"What about bear?"

"Yes, we eat bear. A bear can feed many."

"My great-grandfather was named John Bear Hunter," I told him.

"He must have been a strong brave and a good hunter," Reelfoot said.

I thought of the picture Grandma Cope had shown me of Saffron Cope and John Bear Hunter. He had been a strong brave.

I walked away from the village to the creek where the Indians got their water. I squatted beside it, wrapping my arms around my knees. Scattered snowflakes drifted down. I heard a movement in the trees across the creek, but I wasn't interested. Probably another herd of deer or some chipmunks leaving the area, I thought to myself.

Whinny-ah-haw!

I jumped up. Standing across the creek was our mule! "King George!" I hollered, and ran toward the creek.

Ah-haw! the big mule brayed, and backed away.

I stopped. I didn't want to scare him. "George, it's me. Your good pal Zoey. Are you hungry, boy?" I asked in a quiet, shaky voice.

The mule stood still and looked at me with soulful eyes. I had never seen a more handsome creature in all my life.

I took my shoes off and stepped into the creek. The

water was frigid, but that didn't stop me. I desperately wanted to catch King George before he ran away again. He still wore his bridle with the reins dangling in front, though his packs had disappeared.

I waded through the icy water, holding my dress up around my waist so as not to drench it. The creek wasn't deep, but the water was moving a lot faster than I'd thought. It rushed through my legs and grabbed at me, which was a scary sensation. I remembered Mom saying that a person can drown in a teaspoon of water and that rushing water is the most dangerous. After my experience in the drainage ditch, I believe her. Look where that got me!

"Hang on, George, and I'll give you some grub," I said to the mule.

His ears twitched in reply. He stepped toward the creek.

"That's right, boy, c'mon. Zoey has some corn for you," I said in what I hoped was a voice attractive to mules.

King George stomped his back hoof at me.

I clicked my tongue at the mule. "C'mon, George. Come to Zoey," I said as I reached the other side. I clambered up the creek bank and stopped. Up close, I could see that George was so skinny, his ribs were showing. My heart swelled with love. "You looked for me, didn't you, George," I whispered as I approached him.

Ah-haw, George replied, but his bray sounded weak, not at all like that of the feisty mule I remembered.

I took the dangling rein in my hand. I reached up

and patted King George on the shoulder. "It's all right now, boy. Zoey's here."

In answer, the mule nudged me, hard. I threw my arms around his broad chest and cried into his mangy coat. He was skinny and he stank a bit, but no animal had ever looked as dear to me as King George. After a moment, he stomped his hoof at me again.

"Yes, I promised you lunch, didn't I?" I told the mule. I pulled on his reins and started down the creek bank and into the water. The mule balked. "C'mon, it's grub time," I said to him, and pulled on the reins. George began to follow me into the creek. I tried to hold up my dress with one hand, but most of it dangled in the water. I didn't care. I'd walk through a hundred icy creeks again to see King George and his familiar mule face.

On the other side of the creek, I pulled until George scrambled up and out. Then I picked up my shoes in one hand, and with the reins in the other, I led the mule to the village, talking to him the entire way, catching him up on all that had happened.

When the Indian women caught sight of me in my wet dress and pulling the skinny mule, they laughed in a kindly way. They tied the mule up and gave him corn and grain. He munched away and seemed quite content, I was happy to see.

They gestured for me to remove my wet clothes. Inside one of their lodges, they built up the fire and wrapped a robe around me. A young woman whisked my wet clothes away while another brewed a strong tealike drink. It felt like home, even though it was completely different, of course. But I felt a sameness with these people, a sameness like I feel with Grandma Cope. There is no denying that these people are my ancestors, even if they lived almost two centuries before me. The young women look a lot like Grandma Cope looked in her wedding picture, and the tea tastes the same as the kind Grandma makes for me when I'm sick. And even though we don't speak the same language, I appreciate their kindness, and try to smile and nod a lot to let them know how thankful I am for their help.

"Is my mule okay?" I asked the women. When they looked at me in puzzlement, I tried to think of how to say mule. I summoned my energy and brayed. *"Whinny-ah-haw,"* I said, and nodded.

The women smiled and nodded back. After I drank more hot tea, I drowsed beside the fire, the foreign voices of the women lulling me to sleep. I dreamed I saw Grandma Cope standing in a river. She was beckoning me.

February 6

I awoke to the sound of thunder. Lightning flashed around me and the ground began to tremble beneath me, but not as violently as it had before. I jumped up and ran outside.

The Chickasaws emerged from their lodgings, many of the women screaming and clutching babies. I couldn't understand a thing they were saying, but I got the gist of it from their gestures. They were scared to death! I was, too.

They gathered around Reelfoot. He spoke to them in Chickasaw. I knew that he was telling them to leave the area.

Many of the older Indians shook their heads. I wished I had some way to prove to them that Reelfoot was right, that they should leave their homes, and soon.

The frustration on Reelfoot's face showed that his efforts were futile. Most of the older Chickasaws returned to their lodges. Some of the younger women appeared to be asking him more questions.

Reelfoot pointed at the sky, and he pointed at me. Many people turned to look at me with their bright black eyes. I hoped they wouldn't blame me for their having to leave their homes. Or worse.

After more talk, they were nodding in agreement. Some of the younger women returned to their lodges and came out a few minutes later with babies strapped to their backs, carrying baskets with household items in them. The younger men carried things, too. They were planning to go, it seemed.

Another flash of lightning sent King George dancing around the tree he was tied to, snorting with fear, unable to escape. I wanted to bury my face in his hide and wait it out—not see what was coming—but I could see the mule was frightened out of his mind. His eyes were rolling, the whites clearly visible.

"Wait, boy, wait," I shouted above the growing noise.

I put my hands to the job of untying his reins from the tree. The ground shook beneath my feet. A noise like a freight train bearing down on us thundered in my ears. My fingers trembled.

I tried to calm myself. This was no worse than what I'd already survived, I reasoned. Nothing worse. I just had to wait it out.

Whinny-ah-haw! George brayed.

"Zoey, bring the animal to me," Reelfoot ordered.

"Why?" I asked.

"I want the women to take him."

"No! Not King George! I want him to stay with us," I cried.

"We have no need of him. The women can use him. Bring him to me."

I took King George by his mane and pulled him toward the women. I knew what Reelfoot said was true, but it hurt, more than just about anything I had endured so far. I wasn't ready to let the mule go. It seemed so . . . final. Like my time here was really done.

One of the women patted me on the arm. I looked at her. Strapped to a carrying board on her back was a baby who needed to get to safety. King George was better off with the women than with me.

I gave him a quick kiss on his wide, soft nose. Then I ran from the women, crying. I couldn't help myself. Letting go of George again seemed like the end of the world at that moment.

I turned to look at King George one more time.

Reelfoot was pointing northeast. After a lot of nodding and waving, the Chickasaws who were leaving the area began their journey. Reelfoot looked relieved to see them go.

February 7

When I awoke, I could tell it was dark outside because the inside of the lodge was dim, lit only by the fire. I felt rested and warmed. And hungry. I looked around. A few of the older women who had refused to leave slept nearby. The old baggy dress that Pru had given me was clean and sitting in a pile with my shoes by the fire.

I dressed and pulled on my shoes. Outside, the night was cold. I looked up to see the twin tails of the comet in the sky. The same comet that Grandma Cope had sewn on my journal for my birthday. That seemed like a lifetime ago.

"It is near time," Reelfoot said close to me. My heart jumped in my chest. I hadn't heard him coming.

"Are you sure?" I said. My heart beat like a triphammer. I wrapped my arms around myself.

"Soon," he said, and touched my face.

"But what happens next?" I wiped tears from my cheeks.

"I go to meet the Great Spirit. You will return to your peoples," Reelfoot said. He looked at me for a moment. "Thank you for helping me to save Laughing Eyes," he said. "My children's children's children will thank you someday. The Great Spirit will look favorably upon you, Zoey, for your bravery." He touched my face again.

At the edge of the village, Reelfoot propped his long rifle against a tree stump and began walking westward, toward the river, his head high and his step proud.

"Wait, I'll go with you," I called, and ran after him. I did not want to be alone to face whatever was coming.

We walked a mile or so in silence. I wondered what Reelfoot was thinking. I only hoped that somehow— today—I could get home.

I knew when we had neared the river, even without seeing it. I could hear the rushing waters. Broken trees littered the ground. Reelfoot walked ahead of me, clearing a path for me where he could.

Without warning, the earth shook violently beneath our feet. Reelfoot and I fell. Large fissures opened in the ground. Gases and vapors filled the air with a disgusting odor. I gagged. My eardrums ached with the change in air pressure.

Before too long I couldn't see anything, as the sky turned completely black. The ground pitched and rolled. My stomach did the same. I leaned over and threw up.

Sudden light filled the air. *Lightning.* But it was coming up from the earth, all around me, like nothing I had ever seen before! And with it came an increased bucking of the ground beneath me. In the distance, I heard the roaring of the river. It sounded like it was rushing straight toward us!

I felt cold water splashing across my feet and ankles, growing deeper by the minute. The lightning bolts continued to burst from the ground. I hugged my knees, afraid to look but afraid to close my eyes. The water was getting deeper. I stood up and tried to run, but my wet dress slowed my progress.

I remembered Reelfoot walking calmly westward, toward the river, to face his destiny. I remembered my decision to face my own destiny. I thought of Pru, Grace and the babies, and King George helping the Indian women and their children. I thought of Laughing Eyes and her baby, who would be related to me in the future. I thought of Grandma Cope and my family.

The water was up around my knees now and pulling, sucking at my dress. It felt warmer somehow. No longer icy. I wondered if it was from the electricity.

The water grew hotter as it moved faster. It was getting deeper, too. I continued trying to get away from it, even though I realized the effort was useless—I wasn't ready to give up. As the water reached my waist, my hair began to stand on end.

I knew that I would have to try to swim soon. There was nothing to hold on to. My scalp began to burn. I dropped down under the water in an attempt to cool my head. When I stood up again, the water was deeper.

"Please, God, I don't want to drown," I whispered. The screams of animals fighting the rushing river pierced the air around me. I wanted to scream, too.

For a moment, the flooding seemed to stop. I treaded

water and took huge gulps of air. Maybe it's over, I thought. Maybe I can swim to safety.

Suddenly, I heard Grandma Cope in my head, clear as a bell. *Rivers take us away, and rivers bring us home.*

With a powerful whoosh, the river began rolling backward, pulling, carrying me along with it. I saw a tree approaching fast and closed my eyes, powerless, fearing the impact.

Then nothing.

Prudence

10 February 1812

We are safe and we are with Papa! He was looking for us in New Madrid when it was flooded, so he came north to Fort Jefferson with the refugees. The worst is over, I pray. We are at what is left of Fort Jefferson for now, hoping to regain our strength with the other people who made it here.

But we must soon journey to New Madrid. Papa wants to help rebuild the town. We will live there while he continues his ministry, although he has decided to set up a church in town for the Indians to come to, instead of being away from home so often and long. I intend to look for Zoey, in case . . . in case she did not make it back to her own time.

Our friends the Bryans survived. They have sent word to us that we are welcome to stay with them when we return to New Madrid. I cannot wait to see Lizzie again!

One of the young soldiers here at Fort Jefferson is the

same soldier who doffed his hat at me in New Madrid! His name is William Bradley. He will return to New Madrid, too, where they are rebuilding the fort. I look forward to getting to know him, but for now I am busy helping teach the younger children their lessons. Papa is proud because many of the Indian children are joining us in the schoolroom each day.

The men and women who come into Fort Jefferson bring terrible tales about those who died when the river took New Madrid. Thanks be to God that Papa survived. Others who were as fortunate are already returning and attempting to rebuild on the banks of the Mississippi.

Something else the refugees talk of is the drowning of many of the Chickasaws in Obion. I wonder if Kalopin met his destiny there, as he said he would.

Mama seems to miss Zoey—and Kalopin and Laughing Eyes. I heard her telling Papa about a strange girl who appeared when we most needed help, and about the way Kalopin and his wife helped when the babies came. Papa does not seem to understand completely about Zoey, but he admits he is thankful that we had help. I told Papa that we would not see Kalopin again. Papa did not question this. He still believes it is his calling to minister to the Indians, but he is not as dismissive of their beliefs now—especially since hearing the talk of the devastation in Chickasaw Country. I think that the earthquakes have changed Papa a bit.

I cannot wait to tell Saffron and Lennon about Zoey and our adventures when they grow old enough to understand. Zoey taught me so much about trust. And friendship.

Zoey, dear Zoey. How I miss her!

Zoey

I'm home! I mean, I'm in my own time again. Craziness, I know. I haven't written in a while, because it has been wild trying to get settled back in to modern life. Not that it's been hard to get used to the modern conveniences again, though!

I don't remember a thing that happened after I saw that tree trunk rushing toward my head, but I woke up in a field. It was raining. I got up and walked around. I heard loud noises and wondered if they meant more earthquakes. Then I realized what all the commotion was. It was the sound of traffic—cars whizzing up and down the interstate! So I followed the sounds until I saw an overpass and light poles. I was on the highway going to Reelfoot, about where we must have gotten off the bus during the storm.

And then I saw the oddest thing. A billboard. With my picture on it—but not a very good one. It was from sixth grade. I had no makeup on, and my hair was frizzy. I was standing there in the rain, staring up at that billboard, when cars began slowing down to look at me, then stopping. For me. People got out of their cars and approached me like I was some kind of alien or something.

I saw why later, when I was sitting in the front seat of a lady's van eating a candy bar and drinking a Coke, waiting on the highway patrol and the FBI and everyone. Out of habit, I pulled down her visor and took a quick peek at myself in the mirror.

I looked like a beast. My beautiful, long hair that took me nearly forever to grow? Pretty much gone. Fried off my scalp by the lightning, I guess. And the dress I was wearing, which wasn't all that gorgeous when Pru gave it to me, looked like I'd been sleeping in it for years. No wonder traffic stopped.

But I'm home. Mom and Dad have cried buckets for days on end. The first night, after I talked to a hundred different people in uniforms, and saw some doctors at the hospital where they checked me in for observation, my parents had a long chat with me.

"Zoey," Mom said. "I know you were having a bad time before you . . . disappeared. We blame ourselves!" Mom started to cry. "We were being selfish!"

"I blame myself," Dad said.

"Let's not rehash it." Mom patted Dad's hand.

They both turned to look at me. "We kind of lost sight of what's important for a while, Zoey. We're sorry we put you through that bad time," Dad said.

"We're trying to work things out," Mom said with a small smile. "It's not going to be easy, but we don't want to give up on our family yet."

I thought of why I had gone back in time. "You're right, Mom," I said. "You and Dad can't give up on our family, or me being thrown back to the past was for nothing!"

Mom and Dad looked shocked for a minute. Uh-oh. I knew they'd never believe my story.

Mom laughed nervously. "We're seeing a counselor, and your dad is looking into going back to school and changing careers," she said, as if I hadn't spoken at all.

"Wow, Dad!" I said. I'd go along with them for now, but eventually they would have to listen to me. "What are you going to study?"

Dad smiled. "Meteorology. I think I'd like to be a meteorologist and study weather."

Mom had a proud look on her face.

"That's great, Dad," I said. "Like storms and stuff?"

Dad nodded.

"Mom," I said, "I've never told you, but I think it's awesome that you became a midwife. I never realized how important it is before, but I learned while I was . . . away that what you do is very hard."

At that, Mom looked happy and bewildered at the same time. I understood. I'd felt that way most of the time I was gone.

For the rest of the evening, until they both collapsed in chairs and nodded off, Mom and Dad cried a lot and held my hands and asked me about a hundred times if I was okay.

Strange, though. Grandma Cope hasn't shed a tear. When she came to see me in the hospital, she smiled and hugged me, and she whispered "Thank you" in my ear.

"For what?" I asked.

"For facing your destiny with bravery."

I thought about that. And I remembered Reelfoot saying his children's children's children would thank me some day.

Since I've been home, Grandma's been happy as a clam, singing, rubbing my scalp with some smelly salve that has gosh knows what in it, and making me drink that hot tea like the stuff the Chickasaw women gave me. I asked her, "Do you know who Kalopin was? And Laughing Eyes? And Copiah?"

"Do you?" she returned.

I do.

She showed me her birth certificate. Copiah. "I called myself Cope when I started working—to sound less Indian," Grandma said. "It stuck. I never told your mother because I didn't want her to think I was ashamed. It was just easier."

I knew it! Laughing Eyes lived, and her baby lived, and her family name was Copiah. And by going back into the past and being braver than I've ever been, I helped save Grandma Cope. She says that her great-great-great-and-more-greats-grandmother, way back, was the granddaughter of the Choctaw chief Copiah, and the daughter of the Chickasaw mingo Kalopin—called Reelfoot by the white settlers—and of Laughing Eyes.

"Did you know I would leave you to go back in time?" I asked Grandma Cope.

"I had a vision," she said.

"On Thanksgiving, right?" I remembered her episode before we ate turkey.

"Yes."

"Why didn't you tell me? And why didn't you tell me before how important it was to find out about my family and who I came from?" I asked her.

"It wasn't *my* place to tell you, Zoey," Grandma Cope said. "Just as your parents had to come to their own decisions about what is important to them, you did, too. If I had told you, you might have had even less interest than you did in learning about your heritage."

"And if you'd told me, and I'd told Mom, she never would have let me get on that bus," I said. I remembered Mom talking about her bad feelings about the trip. "But she had some sense that something was about to happen, didn't she?" I asked Grandma.

"Yes, she did. That's why I volunteered to chaperone. I thought it might ease her mind." Grandma smiled at me.

"I thought about that so many times when I was in the past," I said. "I wanted to come home and tell you how sorry I was for hurting your feelings. Do you forgive me?" I wiped away a tear.

"I know you didn't mean to hurt me," Grandma said, and gave me a hug.

But Grandma didn't know anything about Prudence Charity Keeler, or Grace, or the babies. Or King George, maybe the most loyal friend I've ever had, after Pru and Jillian. And Reelfoot, of course.

The sad thing is that Mom and Dad don't believe a word I say. I mean, they don't think I'm lying or anything. But I was gone for almost two months, and telling them I traveled back in time did *not* reassure them. They think I sustained some head injury, and I even heard them whispering about the possibility that I'd been kidnapped, especially considering the granny dress I was wearing when I reappeared. The doctors assured them that except for losing ten pounds, I'm perfectly fine, and in exactly the same physical condition I was in when I disappeared. Of course, I know better. I don't think I'll ever forget what happened to me, and how I saved my family. And found myself.

Oh, oh! Before I forget, here's something I learned from Mike's book, which is now my book, because he gave it to me. In 1820, John Haywood founded the Tennessee Antiquarian Society. It went bust, but the Tennessee Historical Society was established in 1849. And I joined it! Even though I have had a first-class, firsthand lesson in history the last couple of months, a girl can never learn too much about her home state. Or its peoples.

Zoey

Epilogue

A Sunday in April, Present Day

I haven't written in a while. I've been busy getting caught up with my schoolwork. And seeing Mike. Yes, Mike MacPherson is my boyfriend! Who'd believe it, but he's so smart and so much fun. He joined the Tennessee Historical Society with me. And I don't care who knows it.

Anyway, I have to write about what happened today. It seems unbelievable, but then again, after what has happened to me, nothing is too strange to believe.

I was looking around at my family sitting at the table with me after church, and I was feeling pretty good. Mom and Dad sat at either end of the table, like they always used to when we all lived here. They're not completely back together yet, but things have improved on the home front. I was thinking how glad I am that my adventures in the past helped my parents find their way back together.

Across from me sat Grandma Cope. During my time with Pru, Grandma Cope moved in with Mom to help her. Apparently, Mom was a mess. And she's never moved out. This makes me happy, too. I feel like I have a complete family unit again. In transition, yes, but better than before.

The doorbell rang. "That's probably Jillian," I said, about to get up. "She said she was coming by."

"I'll get it, Zoey," Dad said. "Eat your dinner."

I sat back down and put another bite of mashed potatoes in my mouth. That's another huge benefit of my disappearance: lots of home cooking. Everyone wants to fatten me up. I am not complaining. Mom doesn't fix all that tofu and organic stuff anymore. Real meat and potatoes for dinner now. With lots of pesticide-free veggies and fruits, of course.

I turned to listen to Mom telling Grandma Cope about the new support group she was forming for midwives.

"But please, sir, I need to see Zoey," I heard someone saying from the front door. Grandma Cope and Mom fell silent as the voices grew louder. After a minute, Dad returned to the dining room.

"They were persistent," Mom said with a little smile. "Did you convince them to go away?"

"They were more determined than most," Dad said. "They wouldn't leave until I promised to give this to Zoey." He had a quizzical expression on his face as he looked at the object in his hand.

"What is it?" Mom asked. "What do you have?"

Dad handed her a small, rusted, square, flat object. She turned it over and rubbed her thumb across the back.

I leaned across the table. As Mom rubbed harder, the smiling faces and moptops of the Fab Four appeared. Mom's old Beatles mirror! The one I'd given Grace in 1812!

Mom gasped when she recognized the mirror, but I didn't wait to try and explain. I shot up from the table and ran to the living room. Standing on the front porch, looking in our front window, were a woman and a girl about my own age, who had the same reddish blond hair and blue eyes as Pru. Only this girl was dressed in modern clothes.

I threw open the front door and stepped out onto the porch, my heart racing.

"Are you . . . ?" My voice choked off in my throat.

"I'm Saffron Bradley Bryan," the older woman said. "And this is my daughter."

"I'm Zoey. Zoey Prudence Bryan," the girl said. "And you're Zoey, too."

Behind me, Mom gasped. I stumbled a bit and Dad grabbed my arm. "Are you all right? If you're not up for this, honey . . ."

"No, Dad! I mean, yes, I'm fine. I just need to sit down." I let Dad lead me back into the living room and to the couch. The woman and the girl followed us in. Grandma Cope stood in the doorway to the dining room, watching. Dad motioned everyone to sit. The room was quiet.

"How did you know where to find me?" I asked.

"We heard the news about you disappearing on your field trip during the electrical storm," Saffron said, "just like one of our ancestors described in here."

Saffron reached into her large pocketbook and pulled out a smaller leather bag. It looked old. From that, she took a number of items—including Pru's journal—and placed them on our coffee table!

"These things have come down to us through our family, generation after generation, along with the legend of Reelfoot and Zoey."

Mom gasped and covered her mouth with her hand.

"'Please find Zoey and tell her that I lived,'" Saffron read from the journal. "'Tell her that I did meet a few beaux and one special one, a soldier named William Bradley, who became my husband. Tell her that I went to school and became a teacher.'"

I dropped my head into my hands and wept with relief. Pru had lived and had a family of her own. She had become a teacher! Everyone waited until I had stopped crying.

"What about Grace and the babies?" I asked.

"They made it, too," Zoey Prudence said. "Grace, Saffron, and Lennon all made it."

"So Pru's papa was never found?" I asked, sorry for Pru.

"Yes, he found them at Fort Jefferson and they were reunited," Saffron said. "There's more here," she said, turning back to the journal. "'Tell Zoey,'" she read, "'that Laughing Eyes lived, too, as did her daughter, whose name was Copiah after her grandfather.'"

I looked at Grandma Cope, and she winked at me.

"'Tell Zoey that I loved her like a sister. Tell her we

thanked God every day that she appeared in our lives,'" Saffron read.

I started to cry again. It was all too much. Mom and Dad were crying, too.

"Don't cry, Zoey," Zoey Pru said. "It's all right."

"I'm crying because I'm happy," I said. "I've never been so happy in my life."

"Zoey, we were wondering if you'd like to come and visit us in Missouri this summer," Saffron said. "And your parents, too, of course. We'd love to show you all the family things that have been handed down to us from Prudence Charity."

"Oh, Mom, Dad! Can I? Can we go?" Then I stopped short. "Wait, I promised Grandma Cope I'd go to Reelfoot Lake and Chickasaw Country with her this year. She wants to go back to where she came from and see it with me." I looked at Grandma Cope. "And I want to go, too."

"We can do both, Zoey," Grandma Cope said. "If the Bryans don't mind an extra guest. And if you don't mind a chaperone." Grandma's eyes were twinkling.

"I'd love it!" I said.

"And we'd love to have you, Mrs. Cope," Zoey Pru said. Then she turned to me. "I have to warn you, though, we live way out in the boonies. We don't have cable TV or stuff like that. We don't even live too close to a mall."

"We live on a small farm," Saffron explained. "It's been in our family since Pru married William Bradley."

"I want to go!" I said. "I love animals! I love farms. And who cares about TV?"

Mom and Dad laughed at my enthusiasm. "Zoey, what do you know about farms or farm animals?" Mom asked. "Not that I don't think it would be a wonderful experience for you."

"I know about mules!" I said. "Do you have any on your farm?"

"Yeah, we do! He's a stubborn old coot."

"Wow! What's his name?" I asked.

"We call him George," Zoey Pru answered. "After one of Prudence's farm animals—"

"Yeah! I know." I laughed. "King George!"

AUTHOR'S NOTE

The Legend of Zoey grew out of my fascination with the stories my great-grandmother Sweetmama told me about the horrific New Madrid Earthquakes of 1811–1812, the formation of Reelfoot Lake, and the legend surrounding the cursed Chickasaw chief Kalopin. In researching the earthquakes and Reelfoot Lake, two invaluable books I read were *On Shaky Ground: The New Madrid Earthquakes of 1811–1812* (University of Missouri Press, 1996), by Norma Hayes Bagnall, and *The Earthquake America Forgot: 2000 Temblors in Five Months . . . And It Will Happen Again!* (Gutenberg-Richter Publications, 1995), by David Stewart and Ray Knox.

While *The Legend of Zoey* is fiction, the events it is based on—the New Madrid Earthquakes and the formation of Reelfoot Lake—are not, and they changed landscapes and lives forever.

In 1811, settlers called the western portion of the young state of Tennessee Chickasaw Country. The area was populated by a tribe of Indians and a few pioneers who had made their way to what was then the wild frontier of the United States. Across the border in the Louisiana Territory, New Madrid was the first town in what was to become Missouri. It offered trading and worshipping opportunities to many of the settlers in the area, who would travel there for goods and the chance to socialize.

For months before the earthquakes began, there were odd signs or portents—what folks in West Tennessee and the eastern part of the Louisiana Territory thought of as evil omens—of a coming upheaval. A strange two-tailed comet like the one Prudence describes in this story was visible in the night sky in 1811. (The comet in Zoey's time is fictional.) Settlers and Indians noticed animals trekking cross-country in unusual, diverse groups, leaving the area instead of hibernating. Fish tried to jump out of the Mississippi River and up onto its banks.

During the early morning hours of December 16, 1811, people in the area awoke to the terrifying sounds of trees crashing, animals screaming, and the ground exploding beneath their homes. Earthquake!

I tried to imagine how frightening it must have been to experience this earthquake in a time with no electricity or telephones—and no Red Cross or local hospitals to provide emergency help.

For months, the land in Chickasaw Country trembled and shook. People as far away as Boston reported feeling tremors from the quakes. Trees split in half and fell from the force of the bucking land. Sinkholes appeared out of nowhere. Black ooze and hot rocks boiled out of the ground, bringing forth a noxious fog that smelled like rotten eggs.

On February 7, 1812, the largest and most powerful of the earthquakes hit. Seismologists estimate that it would have measured at least 8.8 on the Richter scale, which we use today to measure the magnitude of energy released by a quake. A measurement above 8.0 is considered a great earthquake, with significant destruction and loss of life.

The quake on February 7, 1812, was so strong that it pushed the Mississippi River backward for a brief time, changing its course forever. Islands were submerged. River towns like New Madrid fell into the water and disappeared. As a result of the flooding, a large lake formed in West Tennessee, drowning a village of Chickasaw Indians and other settlers. That lake still exists today.

Reelfoot really was the English name for a Chickasaw mingo (chief) in the doomed village. The Chickasaws called him Kalopin, which means "one who reels," because he was born with a disfigured leg and foot. He limped, or "reeled," when he walked.

According to legend, Reelfoot fell in love with an Indian princess named Laughing Eyes from a neighboring tribe of Choctaw Indians. Laughing Eyes was the daughter of the Choctaw chief, Copiah. When Reelfoot stole Copiah's daughter to be his bride, Copiah cursed Reelfoot and his people. According to Copiah, the earth would destroy itself, and Reelfoot's people would die in a watery grave for the crime he had committed.

Because of the legend surrounding Reelfoot, Laughing Eyes, and her father, Copiah, people in the area called the new body of water Reelfoot Lake. It is not deep, but it is large, covering about thirteen thousand acres. To this day, nearly two hundred years later, the ghostly stumps of cypress trees destroyed during the earthquakes rise above the waters of Reelfoot Lake.

The steamboat *New Orleans* did exist, and it was the first steamboat to travel the Mississippi River. Nicholas Roosevelt built the boat and, along with his pregnant wife, Lydia, took the *New Orleans* on its maiden voyage in the fall of 1811. The steamboat reached New Madrid on December 19 and later stopped at the town of Little Prairie, but the crew would not take on any passengers for fear of capsizing.

Eliza Bryan (Pru's friend Lizzie) did exist, and was working as a schoolteacher near New Madrid, living with her parents and siblings, when the New Madrid earthquakes struck. Four years after the quakes, she wrote an account of her experiences. Later, a Methodist minister named Lorenzo Dow published her writings in a journal. In *The Legend of Zoey* Eliza is a younger girl, called Lizzie.

With my characters Zoey Saffron Lennon Smith-Jones and Prudence Charity Keeler, I tried to portray girls typical of 1811 *and* the new millennium. Young girls on the frontier of the United States often had hard, lonely lives, and they faced physical and emotional challenges we can only imagine. But girls today face unique challenges, too—challenges that are not always made easier by our modern conveniences. I hope that Zoey and Pru exemplify the universal concerns of girls of any age and time: growing up and away from parents, longing for a special friend, noticing boys, wondering about the future—and pondering the past.

ABOUT THE AUTHOR

candie Moonshower's *The Legend of Zoey* won the Sue Alexander Most Promising New Work Award, given by the Society of Children's Book Writers and Illustrators. *The Legend of Zoey* was inspired by the legends her great-grandmother, a Creek Indian born and bred in Tennessee, told her about Reelfoot Lake. An army brat, Candie grew up on Okinawa and in Tennessee and has worked as an operations manager, a résumé writer, and a waitress. "Waiting tables is a lot like writing," she says. "Just when you think you've got things under control, some character comes along and places a special order." Married and the mother of two sons and a daughter, she is pursuing a master's in English literature at Middle Tennessee State University. *The Legend of Zoey* is her first novel. Visit Candie Moonshower online at www.candiemoonshower.com.